"Don't cry."

"I'm not crying!" Anna sniffed.

Oh, hell. Being raised with three brothers by his dad, Brandon didn't have a clue what to do when it came to women. Well, at least not the crying part.

He put a tentative hand on Anna's shoulder. "It's going to be all right."

She shot him a look that told him that was an obvious lie.

"Okay, it's not going to be all right." He put his arm all the way around her. "But it could be worse. We could have been shot."

Still crying but laughing, too, she leaned back to look at him. "You always see the silver lining in every cloud, don't you?"

Not always, but definitely right now with her in his arms.

He hated how good it felt to hold her. Just his luck that the first woman who made him feel like this was not only wanted by the law, but was also his family's sworn enemy.

Dear Harlequin Intrigue Reader,

It might be warm outside, but our June lineup will thrill and chill you!

* This month, we have a couple of great miniseries. *Man of Her Dreams* is the spine-tingling conclusion to Debra Webb's trilogy THE ENFORCERS. And there are just two installments left in B.J. Daniels's McCALLS' MONTANA series—*High-Caliber Cowboy* is out now, and *Shotgun Surrender* will be available next month.

* We also have two fantastic special promotions. First is our Gothic ECLIPSE title, *Mystique,* by Charlotte Douglas. And Dani Sinclair brings you *D.B. Hayes, Detective,* the second installment in our LIPSTICK LTD. promotion featuring sexy sleuths.

* Last, but definitely not least, is Jessica Andersen's *The Sheriff's Daughter.* Sparks fly between a medical investigator and a vet in this exciting medical thriller.

* Also, keep your eyes peeled for Joanna Wayne's THE GENTLEMAN'S CLUB, available from Signature Spotlight.

This month, and every month, we promise to deliver six of the best romantic suspense titles around. Don't miss a single one!

Sincerely,

Denise O'Sullivan
Senior Editor
Harlequin Intrigue

HIGH-CALIBER COWBOY
B.J. DANIELS

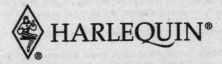

HARLEQUIN®

TORONTO • NEW YORK • LONDON
AMSTERDAM • PARIS • SYDNEY • HAMBURG
STOCKHOLM • ATHENS • TOKYO • MILAN • MADRID
PRAGUE • WARSAW • BUDAPEST • AUCKLAND

ISBN 0-373-88625-X

HIGH-CALIBER COWBOY

Copyright © 2005 by Barbara Heinlein

ABOUT THE AUTHOR

A former award-winning journalist, B.J. had thirty-six short stories published before her first romantic suspense, *Odd Man Out,* came out in 1995. Her book *Premeditated Marriage* won *Romantic Times* Best Intrigue award for 2002 and she received a Career Achievement Award for Romantic Suspense. B.J. lives in Montana with her husband, Parker, three springer spaniels, Zoey, Scout and Spot, and a temperamental tomcat named Jeff. She is a member of Kiss of Death, the Bozeman Writer's Group and Romance Writers of America. When she isn't writing, she snowboards in the winters and camps, water-skis and plays tennis in the summers. To contact her, write: P.O. Box 183, Bozeman, MT 59771 or look for her online at www.bjdaniels.com.

CAST OF CHARACTERS

Anna Austin—She came to Montana determined not to let anyone keep her from the truth—including the cowboy she'd dreamed of for years.

Brandon McCall—The cowboy was just trying to escape his legacy—until he met his destiny one dark night.

Emma Ingles—She had the perfect job, except for the occasional cries she heard coming from the locked wing.

Mason VanHorn—For years he'd hidden the truth about the past. Now someone is digging up those painful memories....

Dr. Niles French—He sold his soul years ago. Now he is old and tired of doing Mason VanHorn's dirty work. But what price will he have to pay to get out from the man's death grip?

Josh Davidson—He would do anything for his boss the doc...even kill.

Lenore Johnson—The private investigator took on the case knowing it might be dangerous. She just didn't realize *how* dangerous.

Dr. Porter Ivers—All he wanted was to comfort his sick wife in her final days. After giving his life to the Antelope Flats Clinic, was a little peace too much to ask?

Dr. Taylor Ivers—An overachiever, she'd followed in her father's footsteps and became the daughter he'd always dreamed of. Or had she?

Sheriff Cash McCall—He had one too many murders on his hands and everywhere he turned, he found his brother in the thick of it.

Chapter One

Saturday night

Emma Ingles loved the night shift. Tonight, she'd fallen asleep watching an old Western on the little TV in the office, her feet up on the desk, her mouth open.

She was a bulky woman, with bad feet and little ambition, who looked much tougher than she was. But she'd found the perfect job for a woman in her late fifties. Well, *almost* the perfect job.

She woke in midsnore. Startled, she sat up, her feet hitting the floor with a slap as she looked around. She muted the movie and glanced at the clock. Just a little after 3:00 a.m.

Listening, she was relieved to hear *nothing*, which was exactly what she should have heard since she was completely alone in the huge old building. At least, she was supposed to be.

Warily, she glanced through the glass-and-mesh window that looked out on the worn linoleum-tile hallway. In the dim light, her gaze wandered down to the chained, locked double doors to the wing that had housed the violent patients, the criminally insane.

Please, not tonight. There were times she swore she heard cries coming from that wing. That's why she kept the TV cranked up loud enough to drown out any noises, real or imagined. The wing had been empty for twenty years now—and locked up tight. If that's where the sound had come from no way was she going down there to investigate—even if she'd *had* a key.

The backdoor buzzer went off, making her jump. That must be what had awakened her. But who would be ringing the buzzer at this hour? Her boss, Realtor Frank Yarrow, was in charge of selling the building and would have called or maybe come to the front door if there were an emergency of some kind.

But she couldn't even see him driving up here at three in the morning. The former Brookside Mental Institution was at the end of a winding dirt road, the monstrous three-story brick building perched like a vulture on the mountainside, ten miles from town. Isolated, hidden, forgotten. For sale.

Given the history of this place, the only people who came up here, especially at night, were kids. They'd get a six-pack and drive up from Antelope Flats, Montana, or from Sheridan, Wyoming, which was about fifteen miles farther south.

After a few beers, they'd dare each other to prove how brave they were by chucking a few rocks through the windows or painting some stupid graffiti on the worn bricks. They never rang the buzzer. Probably because few people even knew it existed.

Emma realized she hadn't heard a car, not that she could have over the shoot-'em-up western on TV with the volume turned up.

The buzzer sounded again. Had to be kids. Some punk kids trying to give her a hard time.

Well, she'd set them straight. She hauled herself up from the chair, picked up the heavy-duty flashlight and opened the door to the dark hallway. Scaring kids was another of the perks that came with the job.

There was only one small light on at the end of each corridor to give the place the appearance of not being completely abandoned. She closed her office door, pitching the hallway where she stood into blackness and waited for her eyes to adjust.

Behind her, there was the faint glow of light coming from her office window that looked out into the foyer. But in front of her was nothing but darkness.

She padded down the gloomy hall to where the building made a ninety-degree turn to the left into another corridor that eventually led to the back door. It was an odd-shaped building, with a wing off each side of the entry that jutted straight back, making a U of sorts behind the place where there had once been an old orchard.

The trees were now all dead, the bare limbs a web of twisted dark wood.

Emma made a point of never going around back. The place was scary enough. That's why she was surprised kids would go around there to ring the buzzer.

Well, they were in for a surprise. She'd give them a good scare. Then she'd go back to sleep.

As she turned the corner and looked down the corridor, she saw that the light at the end had burned out again. But a car with the headlights on was parked outside and she could make out the silhouette of a person through the steel mesh covering the back-door window.

The shape was large. Not a kid. A big man, from the size of him. She felt the first niggling of real fear. What could he want at this hour?

The buzzer sounded again, this time more insistent.

Emma had never been very intuitive, but something told her not to answer the door.

Go back to the office, call the sheriff in Antelope Flats.

She told herself that if the man at the back door had a good reason to be here, he'd have called first. He wouldn't have just shown up at this hour of the night. And he would have used the front door.

She started to turn back toward her office to make that call when she heard what sounded like the front door opening. She froze, telling herself she must have imagined it. She'd checked to make sure the front door was locked before she went to sleep.

Cool night air rushed around her thick ankles. *Someone had come in the front door!*

How was that possible? As far as she knew, there were only three keys: one for herself, one for the Realtor and one for the other night watchman, Karl, the man she was filling in for tonight. The Realtor hated to come out here even in daylight. No way would he be here at this hour!

Until that moment, she'd never considered that anyone who used to work here might still have a key since the locks wouldn't have been changed in the vacant building.

She heard the front door close in a soft whoosh and then footfalls headed down the hall in her direction.

Her fear spiked. She couldn't get back to the office without running into whoever had just come in.

From the quick pace of the footsteps, the person headed her way would soon turn the corner and see her. Panicked, she ducked into one of the empty rooms and immediately realized her mistake. The room was small, rectangular and windowless, with no place to hide.

She started to close the door. It made a creaking sound. She froze, even more shaken at the thought of what she'd almost done. The doors locked automatically with no way to open them from the inside. So even if she hadn't left her keys on her desk in the office, she wouldn't have been able to get out.

She could hear footsteps, close now, and didn't dare move even if there had been enough room to hide behind the partially closed door.

Flattening herself as best as she could against the wall in the pitch-black room, Emma held her breath and watched the dim corridor, praying whoever it was wouldn't look this way.

The footfalls hurried past as the buzzer sounded again. She got only a fleeting look at the man. Tall, dressed in a long black coat, a dark fedora covering all of his hair except for a little gray at the side. She had never seen him before.

The buzzer started to sound again but was cut off in midbuzz. She heard a key being inserted in the lock. The back door banged open.

"I thought I told you not to ring the bell," snapped a voice Emma *had* heard before. The man had called a few days ago. She remembered because no one ever called while she was on the night shift.

He'd demanded information without even bothering to tell her who was calling. She hadn't liked his attitude—that sharp edge of authority she'd always resented.

"I'm sorry, who is this?" she'd demanded, and waited until he'd finally snapped "Dr. French."

He'd asked if anyone was there besides her. She'd told him that was none of his business. Well, did she know what had happened to the patient records? Were they in storage? Or had someone taken them? Could he come up and look for them?

She told him she didn't know anything about any files and no one was allowed in the building at night, that he should talk to the Realtor.

He'd become angry and hung up, but she hadn't forgotten his voice. Or the way he'd made her feel. Small.

"You were supposed to wait," Dr. French snapped at the man at the back door.

"She was starting to wake up and you said not to give her any more of the drug," the other man answered in a deep gravelly voice Emma didn't recognize.

"Get her in here," Dr. French ordered. "Where is the man you said would be here?"

"Karl? Don't know. Haven't seen him yet."

There was a metal clank and then Dr. French said, "You made sure there will be no trace of her?"

"I did just as you said. Got rid of everything. Including her rental car."

Emma didn't move, didn't breathe, but her heart was pounding so hard she feared they would hear it and discover her. They thought *Karl* was working tonight. Because Karl was *supposed* to be working tonight. If she hadn't needed the money when he'd asked her to fill in at the last minute—

"There's a car parked out front," Dr. French said. "It must belong to your friend."

"Guess so, though I thought he drove a truck."

The back door closed in a whoosh, automatically locking. Emma heard another clank and then footsteps coming down the corridor toward the room where she was hiding. Something squeaked as they moved.

Out of the corner of her eye Emma saw the doctor and a large burly-looking man roll a wheelchair past, one of the tires squeaking on the linoleum. The burly man had a bad case of bed-hair, his mousy brown hair sticking out at all angles.

Emma only glimpsed the woman slumped in the wheelchair with her head lolling to one side. She wore a long coat, slacks and penny loafers. Her chin-length dyed auburn hair hid most of her face. She clearly wasn't from around this area.

The wheelchair squeaked down the hall to the echo of the men's footsteps. Emma waited until she heard them turn the corner and start down the hall toward her office before she moved.

Her first instinct was to run down the corridor, out the back door. Except all the doors in the building locked automatically and had to be opened from the inside with a key, a precaution from when patients roamed these halls.

And she'd left her keys on her desk, not needing them to scare away a few kids through the window at the back door.

She would have to hide in the building.

Unless she could get to her keys.

She stole down the corridor, trying not to make a sound. At the corner, she sneaked a look down the hallway toward her office.

The two men had stopped with the wheelchair at the locked section that had once been reserved for the criminally insane.

The chain and lock on the doors rattled. She watched as Dr. French inserted a key. The chain fell away with a clatter that reverberated through the building. Afraid to move, she watched the doctor hold the door open for the wheelchair.

He had a *key?* Even she didn't have a key to that area and had been told it was only a long corridor of padded, soundproof rooms best left locked up.

Emma waited until the men disappeared through the doors, the burly one wheeling the woman into the second door on the right. The number on the door read 9B. What was it she'd

heard about 9B, something terrible. *Oh God.*
She had to get out of here.

If she moved fast, she could get to her office,
get the keys to the front door—and her car. The
doctor had seen it parked out front. He knew
she was here. She had no choice. But if she
could reach her car and get away…

She hadn't gotten but a few yards when she
heard the squeak of the wheelchair; a slightly
different sound echoed. They were already
coming back!

Panic immobilized her. Down the dim hallway, she saw the burly man back out of the
room with the empty wheelchair. She had to
move fast. They would be looking for her, wondering where she was, what she'd witnessed.
After all, she wasn't supposed to be working tonight.

But where could she go? Not the patient
rooms. If they caught her hiding in the dark in one
of them, they'd know she'd heard their conversation.

Where?

She caught sight of the ladies' room just a
few doors up the hall in the same direction as
the men. *Run!* Except she couldn't run. She
couldn't even walk fast because of her feet and
years of inactivity. But she managed a lunging

shuffle, her heart thundering in her chest—a clumsy, terrifying run for her life.

As the doctor came out of the room and closed 9B's door, Emma shoved open the ladies' room door and stumbled into the windowless blackness. Frantically, she felt her way to one of the four stalls.

Stumbling into the cold metal stall, she closed the door, locked it and, quaking with fear, sat down on the toilet.

All she could hear was the pounding of her pulse in her ears and the echo of panting. She had to quit gasping for breath. They would hear her. The place was old and empty. Every sound echoed through it. If she could hear them, they could hear her. She had to get control, had to think.

She held her breath for a moment and listened. The snick of a lock followed the rattle of the chain on the doors to the closed wing. She let out the breath she'd been holding. It came out as a sob. She clutched her hand over her mouth, breathing fast through her nose.

From where she sat, she could see through the crack along the edge of the stall to the lighter gap under the bathroom door.

The empty wheelchair squeaked down the hall along with the sound of the men's footfalls.

She held her breath as a shadow darkened the gap under the ladies' room door. They were directly outside. Had they seen her? Did they know she was in here?

"Looks like Karl's here somewhere," said the burly one. "We interrupted his dinner."

Her sandwich! She'd left it half-eaten on her desk when she'd fallen asleep. She'd also left the light on in her office, the TV on, the volume turned low.

"Karl carries a *purse?*" Dr. French asked in a tone heavy with sarcasm.

Her heart stopped. She'd left her purse on the desk. Her purse!

"Dammit, Davidson, I thought you said Karl was definitely working tonight," Dr. French snapped.

"He *said* he was."

The older man made a disgusted sound.

Emma couldn't hold her breath much longer. Tears burned her eyes. They knew she was in the building. They would look for her. She had to think of something. Some way out of here.

Closing her eyes tightly, she waited. Over the pounding of her pulse, she heard the squeak of the wheelchair growing fainter and fainter as it moved down the corridor away from her.

She waited until she heard the back door

close before she moved. Opening her eyes, she forced herself to leave the stall. A dim light filled the gap under the door. No shadows. She pushed open the door.

They were gone.

She leaned back against the wall, weak with relief.

The hallway was empty.

She heard the sound of the back door opening and closing. A car engine revved, the sound growing dimmer.

Her legs were like water and she feared she might be sick as she shuffled back to her office, trying not to hurry in case anyone was watching her. She didn't look behind her down the hall. Nor did she glance toward the locked wing where the men had taken the woman.

At her partially closed office door, she braced herself and pushed. The door swung noiselessly open. Her heart lodged in her throat as she looked to her chair.

Dr. French wasn't sitting in it, as she'd expected he would be.

The office was empty.

The movie was over on the small TV. Her half-eaten sandwich was still on the edge of the desk along with her Big Gulp-size diet cola and her purse.

She began to cry from relief as she hurriedly closed and locked the door behind her. Stumbling to her chair, she dropped into it, her muscles no longer able to hold her up.

She was safe.

They were gone.

She could pretend she'd never seen them.

But could she pretend she didn't know there was a woman locked in one of the padded, soundproof rooms down the hall? And wouldn't the men return for her?

Emma reached for the remote and shut off the TV. She should call someone. The sheriff. But then she would have to stay here alone until he arrived.

Not if she called from home. She didn't live far from here. Just a few miles down the river toward Wyoming.

She picked up her purse and reached for her kitten key chain with the keys to the doors out of here.

The keys were gone.

Panic sent her blood pressure into orbit. She couldn't get out until she found the keys. She bent, thinking she must have knocked them to the floor.

But as she bent over, the hairs rose on the back of her neck.

In slow motion she lifted her head, then turned by degrees to look behind her through the office window to the hallway.

Dr. French smiled and held up her keys.

Chapter Two

Monday night
Two nights later

Brandon McCall couldn't keep his eyes open. He'd driven every road on this section of the ranch and, like all the other nights, he hadn't seen a thing. Not a track in the soft earth. Not a light flickering down in the sagebrush. Not a soul.

Tonight a storm was blowing in. Lightning splintered the horizon and thunder rumbled in the distance as dark clouds washed across the wild landscape, from the Bighorn Mountains over the rolling foothills to the tall cottonwoods of the river bottom.

The first raindrops startled him, hitting the roof of his pickup like hail. He stopped on a hill, turned off the engine and killed the lights.

Taking off his Stetson, he laid it over the

steering wheel and stretched his long legs across the bench seat, careful not to get his muddy western boots on the upholstery.

He had a good view of the ranch below him and knew there were a half-dozen other men on watch tonight in other areas, waiting for vandals.

Unfortunately there was too much country, and even Mason VanHorn, as rich as he was, couldn't afford to hire enough men to patrol his entire ranch.

Something moved in the darkness, making him sit up a little. A stand of pine trees swayed in the stormy darkness. He watched for a moment, then leaned back again. False alarm. But he didn't take his eyes off the spot.

It looked like another long, boring night since he doubted the vandal was dedicated enough to come out in this weather. This was southeastern Montana, coal country, and coalbed methane gas had turned out to be the accidental by-product of the huge, open-pit coal mining to the south. The thick coal seams were saturated with water, which, when pumped out, produced gas that bubbled up like an opened bottle of cola.

With big money in natural gas, thousands of wells had sprung up almost overnight, causing controversy in the ranching communities. Some landowners had cashed in, opting to have the shallow wells dug on their property. Others, like Brandon's father, Asa, would die before he'd have one on his ranch.

The real battles had less to do with traditional uses of the land and more to do with environmental concerns, though. By extracting the gas from the water, something had to be done with all the water, which was considered too salty for irrigation but was being dumped into the Tongue River. The drilling was also said to lower the water table, leaving some ranch wells high and dry.

Mason VanHorn had the most gas wells and was the most outspoken in favor of the drilling. Because of that, he'd become the target of protesters on more than one occasion.

And that was how Brandon McCall had gotten a night job on the VanHorn spread. He'd been in the Longhorn Café in Antelope Flats the day the new VanHorn Ranch manager, Red Hudson, had come in looking for men to patrol the ranch at night.

Fortunately for Brandon, Red didn't seem to know about a long-standing feud between the VanHorns and the McCalls and Brandon hadn't brought it up. He'd hired on, needing the money. While he worked some on his family ranch at the other end of the river valley, that job didn't pay like this one.

The irony was that his little sister Dusty thought he had a girlfriend and that's why he dragged in like a tomcat just before dawn every day.

He wished. No, this was his little secret. And given the generations of bad blood between the McCalls and the VanHorns, Brandon would be out of a job—or worse—once ranch owner Mason VanHorn found out. He hated to think how VanHorn would take it when he found out he had a McCall on his payroll.

Something moved again in a stand of pines below him. The wind and something else.

He sat all the way up.

A slim, dark figure stood motionless at the edge of the pines. He stared so hard he was almost convinced it was a trick of the light from the storm.

The wind whipped at the trees. Rain slanted down, pelting the hood, pouring down the windshield. He turned on the wipers, squinting into the driving rain and darkness.

This had been monotonous boring work—until last night when several of the wells had actually been vandalized. Nothing serious, just a lame protest attempt, and patrols had been stepped up.

Red had made it clear he wanted the vandal caught at all costs. And now it looked as if the vandal was planning to hit one of the wells in Brandon's section.

The presumed vandal sprinted out from the pines, running fast and low as he wove his way through the tall sage and the rain. He wore all black, even the stocking cap on his head. From this distance, he appeared slightly built, like a teenager. A teenager on a mission, since he had what appeared to be a crowbar in one hand.

The vandal disappeared over a rise.

Brandon slapped a hand on the steering wheel with a curse. If he started the pickup, the vandal would hear it and no doubt take off on him. Brandon needed to catch him in the act.

He had no choice. He was going to have to go after him through the pouring rain and darkness. He'd be lucky if he didn't break his leg or worse, as dark as it was.

Pulling on his coat, he snugged on his Stetson, quietly opened the pickup door and reached back to pull the shotgun from the gun rack behind the seat. Not that he planned to shoot anyone. Especially if it really did turn out to be some teenager with a cause.

But it was always better to have a weapon and not need it than the other way around.

Rain slashed down, stinging his face as he loped down the hillside, winding his way through the sagebrush until he reached the rise where he'd last seen him. In a crouch, the shotgun in both hands, he topped the rise and squinted through the rain and darkness.

At first, he didn't see anything. Coalbed methane wells were fairly unobtrusive. Not a bunch of rigging like oil wells. The wellheads were covered with a tan box about the size of a large air-conditioning unit. The boxes dotted the landscape to the north past the ranch complex, but there were none near the house.

He scanned the half-dozen wells he could see. No sign of anyone. Frowning, he wondered if the vandal might have doubled back, having purposely drawn him away from his pickup. Brandon had been so sure the vandal hadn't seen him where he was parked.

But as Brandon started to look behind him, he caught movement down the hillside toward the ranch house itself and the large stand of pine trees behind it.

The VanHorn Ranch was nothing like Brandon's family's Sundown Ranch, which was family-owned and run with a main house and the barns nearby.

The VanHorn Ranch was run by hired help, so the main ranch house sat back a half mile from a cluster of buildings that housed the ranch office, the bunkhouses and the ranch manager's house.

The rustic main ranch house was long and narrow, tucked back into the hillside and banked in the back by pines. Mason VanHorn lived in the house all alone after, according to local scuttlebutt, his wife had run off and he'd alienated his only two offspring.

The vandal disappeared into the pines at the back of the ranch house, the crowbar glinting in the dim light.

This time of the morning, there were no lights on in the small compound down the road from the ranch house, and few vehicles, since most of the men were out riding the huge ranch's perimeter.

The ranch house was even more deserted since Mason VanHorn had flown to Gillette, Wyoming, two days ago for a gas convention and would be gone for at least another forty-eight hours.

Red had promised a large bonus to any man

who caught the vandals or anyone else trespassing on the VanHorn Ranch before the boss got home.

And now Brandon had one in his sights.

A bank of clouds crushed out the light of the moon. Brandon moved, running fast. Had their vandal gone from wells to an even bigger prize: VanHorn's house?

Brandon reached the trees and stopped, moving slowly through the darkness of the dense pines to the back of the house. The guy was nowhere in sight, but Brandon heard the snap of rain-soaked curtains in the wind and spotted the open window.

He thought about radioing for backup, but just the sound of the radio might warn the intruder. At the window, he raised the glass higher to accommodate his height of six-four, and climbed into what appeared to be a bathroom, since he found himself standing in a large tub, the wet curtains flapping behind him in the wind.

Standing perfectly still, he listened for any sign of the vandal. The bathroom door was open and he could see light coming from down the hall.

Moving cautiously, he stepped out of the tub to the doorway. Across the hall, he could see what was clearly a little girl's room. A spoiled little girl's room, from the frilly canopy bed to the inordinate amount of stuffed animals filling the room. It surprised him, since a little girl hadn't lived in this house in years.

He ventured out into the hall, hoping Mason VanHorn didn't come home early and catch him here. He cringed at the thought of the rancher finding a reviled McCall not only in his house, but dripping on his hall rug.

The flickering faint glow of a flashlight spilled from the last open door on the hallway. He froze, listening. It sounded like someone was opening and closing file cabinet drawers.

He crept toward the sound and the flickering light, moving cautiously, the shotgun in his hands.

As he neared the open doorway, he could hear the intruder riffling through papers, opening and closing desk doors. What was he looking for? Wouldn't a vandal just start tearing up the place? Spray-paint the walls with words of protest instead of going through files?

He stopped as the house fell silent. At the sound of a metallic *tick, tick, tick,* Brandon stepped into the room, the barrel of the shotgun leading the way as he wondered what the vandal had done with the crowbar he'd been carrying. Hopefully he'd left it out in the rain after breaking in through the bathroom window.

The vandal had his back to him, the flashlight beam focused on the dial of a wall safe.

Brandon reached over and hit the light switch. "Freeze!"

The figure froze.

The room was one of those fancy home offices with the massive wooden desk, the expensive leather chair, a nice oak file cabinet and a brushed copper desk lamp with a Tiffany shade. Nice.

The person behind the desk with his back to Brandon was smaller framed than he'd first thought—and from the shape, definitely not a teenager. Nor a man. The hourglass figure was all female and only accentuated by the tight black bodysuit she wore. A long lock of dark hair had escaped the black stocking cap and now hung dripping down her back.

"You caught me," she said in a silken voice as she turned, one hand holding the flashlight she'd had pointed on the safe, the other empty.

She was in her late twenties to early thirties with wide brown eyes, striking features and the kind of innocence that did something to a man.

"Put down the flashlight. Gently," he ordered.

She gave him a look as if she thought he was being overly cautious, but·did as he asked.

"What do you think you're doing?" he demanded.

She blinked. "I was about to open the safe."

"I can see that. *Why* are you breaking into Mr. VanHorn's safe?" he asked impatiently.

Her face was flushed from exertion and wet from the rain, her errant lock of hair soaked. "I wanted to see what was inside?"

"Do you think this is funny?" he demanded reaching for the two-way radio to call this in.

"No," she said quickly. "I'm just nervous. This is the first time I've ever done anything like this."

His hand stopped shy of the radio. "You're in a world of trouble." More than she knew, once he called the ranch manager....

She nodded, a slight tremble of her lips and an edgy flicker of her gaze toward the door giving away her tension. She *should* have been scared since he was holding a shotgun on her, had caught her red-handed trying to break into his employer's safe and she had no way out.

"Do you have to hold that gun on me?" she asked, her big brown eyes wide with fear. "I'm not armed. You can search me if you don't believe me."

It was a nice offer but he shook his head and

swung the barrel of the gun downward away from her. Hell, he could see every curve of her body in that outfit she was wearing. It was time to radio Red Hudson, the ranch manager. His instructions had been quite clear. "No authorities. We handle our own affairs on this ranch."

Resting the shotgun in the crook of his arm, he stepped deeper into the room and unclipped the two-way radio at his hip.

"Please don't call anyone," she pleaded, motioning toward the radio. "I was just out here trying to get a story. I'm a reporter."

He held the radio but didn't press the key to talk. "A reporter?" He hadn't expected that. "Odd way to get a story, by vandalizing and breaking into a man's property."

"I didn't know of any other way since a man like Mason VanHorn, with his kind of power, requires desperate measures," she said. "He can buy all the cowboys he needs to keep his secrets." She gave him a look as if to say he was proof of that.

"Mason didn't buy *me*."

"I thought you worked for him," she said.

"I'm just night security."

She nodded, but clearly believed he was one of VanHorn's henchmen.

Brandon swore under his breath, upset that

she had the wrong impression of him—and yet reminding himself that this woman was a criminal under the law. He didn't have to explain himself to her.

He started to raise the radio.

"What does he pay you?" she asked quickly. "I can't pay you much but—"

"I'm not for hire. Look, if this is your first offense, the judge will probably go easy on you."

She sounded close to tears when she said, "You know if you turn me over to Mason Van-Horn, I will never see the local law, let alone a courtroom."

He hated that she was right. VanHorn would take care of this in his own way. Brandon didn't want to think what the rancher would do to this woman.

"I need to sit down," she said suddenly, and swung her hip up onto the edge of the desk before he had a chance to tell her not to move. "I'm sorry. I can stand if you want."

She slid off the corner of the desk, a movement as graceful as a dancer's. A movement designed to distract, to hide her true intention.

He never saw it coming. Never actually saw her grab the brushed-copper desk lamp. Never saw it in the air until he was forced to raise the shotgun to deflect the blow.

The lamp hit the barrel in a loud clash of metals. The bulb broke, showering him in fine glass. He ducked instinctively as the lamp clattered to the floor and he dropped the two-way radio.

He opened his eyes, feeling the broken glass on his cheeks, wanting to brush it off, but resisting the urge.

He darted a look behind the desk. She was gone. Not that he'd really expected her to still be standing there.

He whirled and rushed to the doorway, the shotgun still in his hands. Stopping at the threshold, he looked both ways down the hall in case she was waiting with another weapon.

The hall was empty.

He rushed toward the bathroom. Would she go out the way she'd come in?

The bathroom was dark. The window still open. The wet curtain billowing in with the wind and rain. He lunged toward the dark opening, determined to catch her. She'd been fast, but he was faster.

He'd only taken a step into the room when he was hit from behind. Pain radiated through his head. She must have been hiding in the room across the hall.

It was his last thought as the white tile floor came up at him just before the darkness.

ANNA HATED that she'd had to hit him and hoped it hadn't been too hard. But he'd given her no choice. She couldn't let him turn her in. Especially before she got what she'd come for.

Hurriedly, she moved back down the hall. She'd found the combination taped under the center drawer of the desk, having discovered a long time ago that men like Mason VanHorn changed their combinations all the time out of paranoia.

But because of that, they had trouble remembering the new combination, had to hide it someplace so it would be handy.

Back down the hall, she stepped around the broken lamp and glass and went to the safe again. She spotted the two-way radio and kicked it behind the curtain.

Starting over after the earlier surprise interruption, she turned the dial, hoping she'd bought herself enough time to finish what she'd started. She began to dial in the numbers she'd memorized.

She'd known she might get caught in the house tonight. There was always that chance. But she'd never dreamed the man holding the gun on her would be Brandon McCall.

She tried not to think about him lying on the floor in the bathroom. She was angry enough to hit him again. And to think that at one time she'd had fantasies about the kind of cowboy Brandon McCall would grow up to be. Definitely not a cowboy doing Mason VanHorn's dirty work.

The tumblers thunked into place and after a moment, the safe door swung open. She heard a groan from down the hall in the bathroom and was glad he was alive, but sorry he was coming around already. She hadn't wanted to kill him, just keep him out of her hair; if she could just finish here and get away without having to hit him again—or him shoot her.

Standing on her tiptoes, she peered into the safe debating whether to take everything or try to go through it here and chance getting caught again.

The question turned out to be moot. She stared into the cold dark cavity. The safe was empty. Not just empty, but dusty inside except for the spot where there'd been something. Unfortunately, that something was gone.

Another groan from down the hallway.

Tears burned her eyes. Mason VanHorn had moved the papers. She was too late.

She turned, blinded by hot tears of anger and frustration, and started out the door. A thought stopped her. She hurried back to his desk. Earlier she'd searched it, the desk drawers and the file cabinets, but hadn't found what she was looking for.

Now she picked up the phone and hit redial on a hunch. If he'd taken the precaution to clean out the safe, he might have taken other precautions, as well.

After four rings, a voice mail message picked up. "You've reached Dr. Niles French. Leave a number and I'll get back to you."

Dr. French. She clutched the phone, sick to her stomach. She heard stirring down the hall. Another groan. *Move. Get out. Now!* Fear paralyzed her. Dr. French.

A groan down the hall.

Hurriedly, she scribbled down the phone number on the display, her hands shaking. If the last call Mason VanHorn had made was to Dr. French, then she knew she was in trouble.

Suddenly she couldn't breathe. She thought she might pass out if she didn't get out of this room. Out of this house. She could hear more stirring down the hall in the bathroom. He was coming around.

She couldn't go out that way. She moved to the window at the far side of the desk, fumbled the lock open and lifted the frame. Kicking out the screen, she shoved a leg out and climbed up, teetering on the windowsill for a moment, waiting for her eyes to adjust to the darkness before she dropped to the ground.

Footsteps in the hall. *Hurry!* She practically threw herself out the open window, hit the wet slick ground and fell, her leggings instantly muddy and soaked.

Scrambling to her feet, she ran through the pouring rain to the lofty pine trees and the cover they afforded. She streaked across the grassy hillside to the creek bed and the cottonwoods. Following the creek, she ran to where she'd hidden her vehicle earlier. She didn't look back, afraid she'd see Brandon McCall's handsome face—and his shotgun pointed at her heart.

She was soaked to the skin and chilled as she climbed behind the wheel, started the engine and peeled out. All she wanted right now was to get back to the motel and climb into a tub of hot water. She didn't want to think about the empty safe. About the call to Dr. French. She didn't want to think about what she'd learned tonight about Mason VanHorn. Or Brandon McCall.

Her hands were shaking as she drove as fast as she could toward the highway, needing to put distance between her and the VanHorn Ranch.

She shouldn't have been surprised. Not about

Mason VanHorn. Or about Brandon McCall. But she was. She'd thought she'd seen something promising in Brandon McCall years ago, but it seemed she had been as wrong about him as she was Mason VanHorn.

Slamming her hand down on the steering wheel, she warned herself not to let this get personal. She laughed at the thought. After years of specializing in digging up dirt, she was good at what she did. She'd written the book on detachment when it came to her job—to her life.

But this wasn't just any investigation. And she could no longer pretend it was. It had suddenly gotten damn personal.

At the two-lane highway, she turned south on the road from Antelope Flats, Montana, to Sheridan, Wyoming. Since her arrival, she'd seen little traffic on this stretch, even in the daytime, except for an occasional coal mine or gas worker, a rancher heading for Sheridan or a fisherman coming up from Wyoming headed for the Tongue River Reservoir. But nobody at this hour of the night.

She watched her rearview mirror expecting to see at least one set of headlights behind her on the rain-slick highway. Instead there was only darkness. At least for the moment. The storm snuffed out all light from the moon or stars, turning the Tongue River to pewter as it followed her over the border into Wyoming.

Her plan had worked, for all the good it had done her. Vandalizing the coalbed methane wells had gotten everyone away from the ranch house. Well, almost everyone.

At least it had gotten her what she wanted—inside the ranch house—inside the safe.

Tears burned her eyes. If Mason VanHorn had cleaned out the safe, did that mean he'd destroyed the evidence? Did that mean she'd never be able to get to the truth?

She rubbed a hand over her wet face and stared past the clacking windshield wipers at the rainy highway. Exhaustion pulled at her. She was wet and tired and cold and discouraged. She'd almost gotten caught tonight, but the fact it had been Brandon McCall made it all the worse.

He hadn't recognized her, she knew she should be thankful for that. But even that hurt. He hadn't remembered her. But she'd remembered him. That should have told her everything she needed to know. Obviously he hadn't been as taken with her as she had been with him all those years ago.

She'd thought about what it would be like to run into him. Just not on the VanHorn Ranch. Not working for the enemy. The long-running feud between the McCalls and the VanHorns aside, she'd expected better of him.

She crossed the river as the highway meandered to Sheridan, Wyoming, fighting her disappointment. Angry with herself for ever thinking he might be different from other men she'd known. Even more angry that, over the years, she'd held him up as the kind of man she would want in her life.

How ridiculous was that? He'd been little more than a boy. She couldn't know what kind of man he would grow into. But she thought she'd known. Obviously she'd seen something in Brandon McCall that hadn't existed.

She felt sick. Men just kept letting her down. What did that say about them? Or her?

How she would have loved to drive straight to the airport and fly home. But she couldn't leave. Hers wasn't the only life at stake here and this wasn't the first investigation where she'd run into trouble. She was known for hanging in until she got what she was after.

Even if she could have let Mason VanHorn get away with what she knew he'd done, she had Lenore Johnson to think about. When she'd hired the private investigator, she'd warned Lenore how dangerous this was going to be.

Now Lenore was missing. Presumed dead, if

Mason VanHorn or Dr. French found out that she'd been asking questions about them.

If Lenore Johnson had failed, Anna knew she had even less chance of finding out the truth. But she had to try to find Lenore, try to help her if she was still alive. How, though, could she find out the truth with everything—and everyone—against her?

Along with Brandon McCall, every ranch hand at the VanHorn Ranch would be looking for her now, including Mason VanHorn himself once he returned from Gillette.

She glanced in the rearview mirror again. Nothing but rain and darkness behind her. The same in front of her. She hadn't been followed. But she wasn't safe. She wouldn't be safe and she couldn't help Lenore until she could get the goods on Mason VanHorn. She desperately needed leverage. She'd thought she would find it in his office safe, that he would keep it where he could get to it, that he needed it as desperately as she did.

If she was right, then the evidence was at the house—just not in the safe. She would have to go back. Tomorrow night, once it got dark.

She'd have to get back into that house, even knowing that they'd all be waiting for her. All the ranch hands and hired thugs. Mason Van-

Horn, if he heard about tonight—and Brandon McCall.

And if she was really unlucky, the man she feared the most, Dr. French.

Chapter Three

Tuesday

Sheriff Cash McCall had just gotten to his office when the phone rang.

"This is Johnson Investigations in Richmond, Virginia," said a woman with a wonderful Southern accent. "I'm calling in regard to Lenore Johnson. She is in your area on an investigation and we haven't received word from her for several days. She had made a prior arrangement to call yesterday afternoon at a set time. She did not call. We have reason to believe she might have met with foul play."

An investigator all the way from Virginia? "I can't file a missing person's report for forty-eight hours on an adult, but I would be happy to take the information," Cash told her.

"We'd appreciate that. Because of the nature of our business, I'm afraid I can't give you the details of the investigation. However, I can tell you where she was staying, the make and model of the car she was driving and give you her description."

"All right." Had she been a tourist, Cash wouldn't even have done that much in the first forty-eight hours. Usually people just lost track of time and forgot to call. But since she was an investigator… And since he was a nice guy who had taken this job to help people…

"She was staying at the Shady Rest Motor Inn in Sheridan. The rental car was a dark green Dodge Dakota, license MT 3-178649. Ms. Johnson is forty-six years old, five-foot-seven, auburn hair, chin-length, slim build, brown eyes. She was armed."

"This investigation," Cash asked. "She considered it dangerous?"

"Yes."

"And that's all you can tell me."

"At this point. If we haven't heard from her in forty-eight hours, I will be happy to disclose additional information. That will give me time to contact our client."

"Your client? Who you also can't divulge at this point," Cash said.

"That is correct."

He groaned inwardly. "But you'll call me if you hear from her."

"Of course. At once. We greatly appreciate your assistance, Sheriff." She gave him her number and hung up.

Cash called information in Richmond, Virginia, and asked for Johnson Investigations. Same number as the woman had given him.

He had just hung up when he got the call from the Antelope Flats Clinic. He was surprised—and instantly worried—when he heard Dr. Porter Ivers's stern voice.

"You might want to come down here," the elderly doctor said….

BRANDON WAS SITTING UP on the gurney at the Antelope Flats Clinic when his brother came in.

"How's the head?" Cash asked.

Brandon swore under his breath. Dr. Ivers must have called him after Brandon had come stumbling in, bleeding all over the floor.

"Better." His head hurt like hell. But nothing like his pride.

"You weren't in that bar fight out at the Mello Dee, were you?" Cash asked. "I'm looking for the guys who tore up the place last night."

"Nah." If he told Cash about last night, he'd

have to tell him about the night security job at VanHorn Ranch. He already knew his brother's response to that.

Nor could Brandon tell him about the vandalisms out there since VanHorn hadn't reported them. As sheriff, Cash would have to pay Mason VanHorn a visit, demanding to know why he hadn't been called—and warning VanHorn not to take the law into his own hands.

Once Brandon's name came up, VanHorn would be beside himself to think he'd had a McCall working for him. Heads would roll. And Brandon—if not shot—would be out of a job. And the VanHorns and McCalls would be at it again.

But Brandon didn't kid himself. None of that was why he couldn't tell his brother. This was about salvaging some of his pride and that meant getting the vandal in his sights again. Hell, he'd been so close to her that he'd smelled her perfume, seen the hint of perspiration on her upper lip, knew the exact shade of her honey-brown eyes.

Unfortunately, he'd fallen for her helpless reporter act and had a sore head to prove it.

If he told Cash the truth, he'd never get a chance to catch the woman. And he *would* catch her. He was counting on seeing her again. His gut told him she hadn't left town, that even though she'd gotten into the safe, she wasn't finished with Mason VanHorn. And this time, Brandon would be waiting for her.

"So how'd you get your head bashed in?" Cash asked. He had his sheriff face on, which Brandon knew meant he'd keep at it until he got the truth out of him. Or something close.

"It was stupid," Brandon said sheepishly, looking down at the floor. He'd perfected this look over the years after getting caught in countless shenanigans. All the McCall boys got into trouble. It was almost a tradition. And as the youngest McCall male, he'd had to sow his share of oats, as well. But at thirty-three, he was taking the longest to straighten up.

He looked at the floor and said, "There was this bull out in a pasture and there was this woman…"

Cash groaned. "You were showing off. This woman have anything to do with why you've been staying out all night for days on end?"

"'Fraid so."

Cash shook his head but smiled. "Our little sister thinks it's serious."

It was serious all right. Just not in the way eighteen-year-old Dusty thought. "Yeah, that

Dusty's a real authority on romance," Brandon quipped.

"Doc says you don't have a concussion."

"Just a few stitches," Brandon said, trying to play it down.

"Twelve is more than a few. What'd you hit?"

"Must have found the only rock in the field when I came off the bull," Brandon said. "But, hell, big brother, you had more stitches than that when you were young."

"When I was *young?* I'm only a few years older than you. And I can still kick your butt."

Brandon grinned. "Might have to see about that someday." He quickly changed the subject. "Heard Molly's back from visiting her mom in Florida." Molly was the woman his brother had fallen in love with and from what Brandon had seen, Cash was more than serious about her. "Is that weddin' bells I hear? Bet Shelby's already bought a mother-of-the-groom dress for the wedding."

Shelby was their mother, but after not being part of their lives for more than thirty years and suddenly returning, her five now-grown children couldn't bring themselves to call her mother.

"You tryin' to change the subject?" Cash asked, eyeing him.

"I don't want to talk about my love life, okay?" His nonexistent love life, especially.

"Neither do I," Cash said. "You want me to call J.T. and tell him you won't be doing any work at the ranch today?"

"That would be great," Brandon said, sincerely touched. Cash was offering the equivalent of an olive branch. "You know J.T. He'll think I busted my head open on a rock only to get out of work."

Cash returned his smile. Their oldest brother, J.T., could be a little intense when it came to the ranch. But J.T. had mellowed some since his recent marriage. A woman was exactly what J.T. had needed.

"With Rourke back, they should be able to manage without you for a few days," Cash said.

Brandon grinned, seeing that his brother was getting him a few days off to recuperate—and spend time with his lady. "You romantic, you. You're okay, Cash, no matter what the rest of the family says about you," he joked.

"I got work to do," Cash said, and turned to leave.

"Thanks," Brandon said to his brother's back. He felt a little guilty about keeping things from Cash. But not guilty enough to confess just yet.

Once he caught the woman from last night, he'd collect his bonus and tell Cash everything. Once VanHorn got wind of everything, the job would be over anyway.

Dr. Ivers came back into the emergency room. He had a frown on his face, as if disgusted with the whole bunch of McCall boys. He'd been stitching up McCall boys from long before Brandon was born. The doc had tried to retire but couldn't seem to make it stick and was only becoming more cantankerous. Kind of reminded Brandon of his father. But then Asa McCall had always been cantankerous and just plain hard to get along with.

That is until recently, when his wife Shelby returned from the dead. Brandon shook off the thought. He didn't want to think about what was going on between his parents.

"You're free to go," Dr. Ivers said, handing Brandon a prescription for painkillers. He checked the bandage on the back of Brandon's head, adding, "I don't want to see you back in here. Don't you have something better to do that get banged up in the middle of the night?" He shook his head again. "Good thing you McCalls are a hardheaded bunch."

"Thanks, Doc," Brandon said, reaching for his cowboy hat. He placed it gingerly on his head, wincing a little.

"You're going to have a scar," said a female voice from the doorway.

"Won't be my first scar," Brandon said with a grin. "Hi, Taylor."

"That's Dr. Taylor Ivers to you," the old doc snapped. Taylor was Dr. and Mrs. Porter Ivers's surprise late-in-life child. She had followed in her father's footsteps, something that Brandon could see pleased the old doc greatly.

Taylor held out her hand. "Hello, Brandon." He took it, not surprised by her firm handshake. She was all business. He hadn't seen her since she was a skinny kid with braces and glasses. She hadn't changed that much, except she had perfectly straight teeth and must have worn contacts.

She'd been one of those gifted kids who went to a special private school, graduating high school at fifteen, college at eighteen and medical school at twenty-two. Last he'd heard, she'd done her residency at some cutting-edge hospital down south.

"You planning to take over for your dad?" he asked her, joking.

"She has bigger fish to fry," Dr. Ivers snapped. "She's not getting stuck here."

"I'll be staying for a while," Taylor said, glancing at her father. "My mother isn't well."

"I'm sorry," he answered quickly.

"I want to be near my parents right now," Taylor said, and turned to her father, "You have a phone call."

"I'll take it in my office." He looked at Brandon. "I'd tell you to take it easy, but I know it would be a waste of breath." The old doc turned and left without another word.

As Brandon slid off the gurney and headed for the door, Taylor busied herself putting away the equipment her father had used to patch him up.

Brandon left with only one thing on his mind—the woman who'd wounded his pride. The flesh injury would heal.

ANNA'S ATTEMPTS to find out if Brandon McCall had been taken to the Antelope Flats Clinic had failed miserably.

As an investigative reporter, she knew a few tricks for getting information. But the woman she spoke to at the clinic, a Dr. Taylor Ivers, wasn't falling for any of them.

Anna hung up, hoping McCall was all right. She'd hit him with a cast-iron cowgirl doorstop. Her disappointment in him aside, she hoped it hadn't hurt him too badly.

She stepped out onto the deck overlooking the Tongue River Reservoir and rubbed the back of her neck, angry with herself for worrying about him. He worked for Mason VanHorn! That should tell her what kind of man he was. More than likely, he deserved anything she gave him.

The morning breeze whispered in the pines and rippled the water's green surface below her into a glittering chop. She could see a half-dozen boats along the red cliffs of the lake and wished she were on the water.

Closing her eyes, she breathed in the smell of the lake and almost thought she felt a memory stir her. She and her father fishing in a small boat, just the two of them, on a summer day, the soft slap of the water against the side of the boat, the steady thrum of the motor, the pull of the rod in her hand.

She knew it couldn't possibly be a memory. She'd never gone fishing with her father. She'd barely known him. At her first boarding school, she'd told everyone that her parents were both dead. In a way, it was true. They were both dead to her.

Going back inside the cabin, she wondered

why she hadn't thought to rent a cabin on the lake in the first place. Staying at a motel, even in Sheridan, Wyoming, even miles from the VanHorn Ranch, had been risky. Here on the lake at this time of year, she could blend in.

In a few hours, when it warmed up, the lake would be alive with the whine of boat motors roaring around, the smell of fires from the campground across the water and wonderful sounds of laughter and voices.

And according to the records she'd uncovered, just down the lake was a piece of recently acquired land that was now part of the VanHorn Ranch. Not exactly lakefront property in the true sense. It was swampy, with lots of trees standing knee-deep in the water with the lake up. The land wasn't used for anything except the wild horses Mason VanHorn had collected before there were laws preventing it.

This morning, after a sleepless night, she'd come up with a plan. Unfortunately, she could do little until almost dark and she'd never been good at waiting.

She tried her cell phone and still couldn't get any service in this remote part of the state. Giving up, she picked up the phone in the cabin and dialed the Virginia number.

"Johnson Investigations," a female voice answered.

"I'm Anna Austin—"

"Ms. Austin, I'm sorry but if you're calling for Lenore, she still hasn't called in. As a matter of fact, we have contacted the sheriff in Antelope Flats."

"That's why I'm calling. I wanted to give you my permission to reveal the nature of her business here and who she was working for," Anna said. "I'm worried about her."

"We're concerned, as well, but the sheriff said no missing person's report can be filed for forty-eight hours," the receptionist said. "He has agreed to keep an eye out for her but can do nothing more at this point."

Forty-eight hours. "I'm going to do my best to find her in the meantime." She gave the receptionist the number at the cabin and hung up.

She had hired Lenore Johnson to verify some information she'd received. Lenore had called two days ago to say that at least some of the information was correct. She hadn't wanted to discuss the case over the phone, adding she had another lead to check out before she flew back. Anna had told her she would be flying out and Lenore had given her the name of the motel where she was staying in Sheridan, Wyoming.

But when Anna reached Sheridan, she'd discovered that Lenore had left the motel without checking out, taking everything with her, and hadn't been seen since.

Anna's gaze went to the manila envelope where she'd dropped it beside the phone. The letter inside had been lost in the mail for nine years.

A part of her wished it had stayed lost.

Sitting down, she picked up the envelope and pulled out the single sheet of paper from inside. The barely legible words had been written in a trembling feeble hand. An elderly woman's deathbed confession.

At first, Anna had thought the woman must have been senile. None of it could be true.

But she'd been wrong. At least some it was true, or Lenore Johnson wouldn't be missing.

Carefully, Anna slipped the letter back inside the envelope and, getting up, hid it under the cushion of the chair. She knew she was being paranoid, but it was the only evidence she had. Even if it was worthless in a court of law without proof to back it up, she didn't want to lose it.

Had the private investigator found the proof? Or had she just asked too many questions?

Anna shivered, hugging herself as she thought of Lenore Johnson. Lenore had known going in just how dangerous this was, and she was trained for this kind of trouble. If *she* had failed...

Anna knew she was completely out of her league. Not that she would let that stop her. Nothing could stop her. She would find out the truth, because she knew it was still on that ranch. Too many people had been involved in the cover-up. Mason VanHorn couldn't be sure the others would keep quiet. He would have evidence he could use to ensure they would never talk. He would keep that evidence close to him, so if all else failed, he could get it and destroy it. If it came to that. She didn't think he felt *that* threatened yet.

So the evidence had to be in the ranch house. She had to find it and she couldn't count on him being gone for long. Once he heard about the break-in, he might come back. Or he might just put more guards on the house, assured that he could protect himself and the evidence.

She had to get back into that ranch house. Only this time, she would need a major diversion—something more than vandalizing a few wellheads.

And this time, everyone would be looking for *her* after Brandon McCall told them what she looked like. At least he didn't know her name. Nor would she be easy to find.

As she looked across at the marina, she knew she had just raised the stakes and was about to gamble everything. There was no turning back now, no matter who got in the way. Even Brandon McCall.

She *would* find out the truth. Even if it destroyed them all.

MASON VANHORN PICKED UP the broken lamp in his office and hurled it across the room. It crashed into the wall, dropping with a clatter.

Red Hudson winced but had the good sense not to say a word. The ranch manager had noticed tracks in the mud behind the house, had investigated and called him. Mason had driven home at once, disbelieving that anyone would be stupid enough to break into *his* house. When he got his hands on the bastard—

"They came in through the window in the bathroom," Red said behind him. "Had to know you weren't going to be home."

"They?" Mason turned to look at him. Red was a big man with a shock of bright red hair, thus the nickname. Mason knew he could count on Red's loyalty because he had just enough on the man to ensure Red would never turn on him.

But unfortunately, Red had a little something on him, as well, which meant he couldn't control him like he could the other men. Red could be pushed, but Mason wasn't sure how far.

"I found two sets of tracks coming and going," Red said. "One could be a small man. The other large."

"I thought you hired extra men to make sure the ranch was secure," he snapped.

Red nodded. "But we were expecting the wells to be hit, not the house."

"If that's your excuse—"

"It's not an excuse," Red said, an edge to his voice.

Mason opened one of the file cabinets, then slammed it. "You're saying there are two vandals?"

Red shook his head. "This isn't the work of a vandal. The house wasn't torn up. These guys were looking for something."

Mason didn't look at him.

"Why do I get the feeling you know what they were looking for?" Red swore. "If I'd known the house might be hit, I would have put some men on it. Whatever was in the safe—"

"It was empty."

Red shook his head. "So you knew they were coming."

Mason didn't have to explain himself to anyone. He'd cleaned out the safe as a precaution. He'd never dreamed anyone would actually break into the house. He wanted to turn his fury on Red, to fire him, to send him packing, but he knew this wasn't Red's fault. It was his own.

Moving to the desk, he stared down, suddenly afraid he might have left something incriminating lying around. Living alone, with no one having access to his office, had made him careless, he realized.

"I want guards around the house until further notice," he ordered. "I want those bastards caught and brought to me."

Red met his gaze. "You think they'll come back?" he asked in surprise.

"Just do it and stop questioning me," Mason snapped.

The ranch manager nodded slowly. "I'll put my best men on the house. But if you really want to catch them, you need to go back to Gillette. If they have a reason to hit the house again, they won't be foolish enough to do it with you here."

Mason couldn't argue Red's logic but he had no intention of going anywhere. "I'll make everyone think I've gone back to Gillette, but I intend to be here tonight when they come back."

"Suit yourself, but it could be dangerous."

Mason laughed. "Only for the bastards who broke into my house."

"It would make my job easier if you'd tell me what they're looking for."

"What makes you think I want to make your job easier? And get someone to clean up this mess." Mason turned and stormed out of his office.

Something caught his eye from down the hall. A drop of blood on the carpet. He felt a chill. Was it possible one of the burglars had been hurt breaking in? He knelt down to inspect the spot. It was right in front of his son's open bedroom door.

He still thought of the room as Holt's even though his son would never use it again. He'd heard rumors that Holt was in California, Florida, even Alaska. He didn't care where he was as long as he never had to lay eyes on him again. His own son had stolen from him— shamed him.

He clenched his fist at the memory. He'd built everything for Holt, his only son, the heir who would one day take over the vast empire he'd built. Now Holt was gone and Mason had seen to it that his son would never get a penny.

He closed the bedroom door. He should have cleaned it out the moment he learned of Holt's betrayal. Should have had everything in it burned.

He moved down the hall, following the droplets of blood and stopped at his daughter's bedroom door, seeing at once that things weren't as they should have been.

One of the stuffed animals on the bed had been moved. He knew because that rag doll had been in the same place for the past twenty years—exactly where Chrissy had left it.

That stupid part-time housekeeper he'd hired must have moved it when she cleaned the room. He'd have Red fire her.

He stepped to the bed, picked up the rag doll. Honey. That's what Chrissy had called it from the day he'd given it to her. He brought the doll to his face, smelled it as if he thought Chrissy's baby-girl scent would still be in the worn fabric. But of course, it wasn't.

He put Honey back where she belonged— between the teddy bears—and tried to picture his precious daughter in this room, but it was too heartbreaking.

"Mr. VanHorn?"

He turned from the room, practically fleeing down the hall to where Red stood, giving orders on the phone to whoever was doing the clean-up.

"I found some blood," Mason said the moment Red got off the phone.

The ranch manager nodded. "There's some on the bathroom floor and the windowsill, too.

One of them must have gotten injured breaking in."

What had happened here last night? "Who did you have watching the wells behind the ranch house?" Mason asked.

"One of my best men. Brandon McCall."

Mason couldn't speak. He started shaking so hard he thought he was having a seizure. Brandon McCall was working security on *his* ranch? A McCall on VanHorn soil? "Fire him immediately!"

"He's one of my best men," Red said, staring at him in stunned surprise.

"He's a *McCall*." It had never dawned on Mason to tell Red never to hire a McCall. But more to the point, what the hell would a McCall be doing working on this ranch? Only one explanation presented itself. "No. Don't fire him. Bring him to me. Now!"

He stormed back down the hall to the bathroom, stooping to pick up the iron cowgirl doorstop on the floor. As he lifted it, he saw the dried blood. "Get me McCall," he yelled back at Red, feeling as if he still might have that seizure.

HEAD ACHING, Brandon set out to find the woman vandal. He started in Antelope Flats, cruising down Main Street, keeping his eye out for her. Antelope Flats was a tiny western town in the corner of southeastern Montana. Tiny and isolated, just the way he liked it.

He'd been born here and lived his whole life on the family ranch north of town. This was his stomping grounds and he knew this part of the country better than anyone. If the woman was still around, he'd find her.

Not that he expected to see her walking down the street. She was much too smart for that. But he thought he might see her car. He'd picked up an accent last night that he couldn't place, but one thing was clear: she wasn't from around here. That meant she was driving either a car with out-of-state plates or a rental car.

There were a few vehicles in front of his sister-in-law's Longhorn Café, the only café in town. But he recognized all of them. Most were pickups, since Antelope Flats was born a ranching town. A few of the trucks were from the coal mine down the road, tall antennae with red flags on top so they could be seen in the open-pit mines.

Antelope Flats had only one motel on the edge of town, the Lariat. He drove out there, but wasn't surprised to see that the parking lot was empty. Anyone who had stayed here last night was already gone.

He found Leticia Arnold in the apartment at the back of the office making what smelled like corncakes.

She saw him and motioned for him to come into the kitchen. "Want some pancakes?"

"No, thanks." Leticia was his sister Dusty's best friend. After high school graduation, while Dusty had opted to stay and work the ranch, Leticia had taken over running the motel so her elderly parents could move to Arizona. Leticia had been a late-in-life baby, the Arnolds' only child.

"I'm looking for a woman," he said, pulling up a chair as she sat down in front of a tall stack of corncakes. Leticia was thin as a stick with a wide toothy smile and all cowgirl.

She grinned up at him. "Do you know how long I've waited for you to say that?"

He laughed. He liked Leticia's sense of humor. "I'm too old for you."

"Shouldn't I be the judge of that?"

He reached over and took a bite of her pancakes. "Wow, you're a pretty good cook. Maybe I'll reconsider," he joked.

"You wish. You're right, you're too old for me," she said, trying to sound disappointed.

"You probably have some rodeo cowboy you've got your sights on anyway," he said.

She looked surprised. "Did Dusty tell you that?"

He laughed and shook his head. His sister Dusty never told him anything, but he knew that the two friends had been hitting every rodeo within driving distance and he doubted they were going there for the fried bread.

He described the woman he'd seen last night as Leticia ate her pancakes and then got up to cook a few more.

"She didn't stay here, but there are tons of motels down in Sheridan you could try. What happened to your head?"

"I thought I was smarter than I was."

She laughed. "I could have told you that and saved you a lot of pain." She put the last batch of corncakes onto a plate. "So this woman made a lasting impression on you and yet you don't know where to find her?" She laughed. "A bad-boy McCall chasing a woman? She must really be something."

If you considered a scar on the back of his head a lasting impression. "Let's just say I'm looking forward to seeing her again."

"Then you're going to need your strength," she said, sliding the plate of pancakes over to him. "Dusty told me that you had a woman in your life."

"Did she now," he said, seeing that Leticia was just dying to call his sister and tell her he'd been by asking about a woman. No way around that. Let Dusty think she was right and that he'd fallen in love. Better than the truth.

SHERIFF CASH MCCALL made a few calls to Sheridan about the private investigator. He'd just hung up when he got a call from the Wyoming Highway Patrol.

"We've got a body just over the state line a few feet," the patrolman said. "Looks like she's yours since she's in Montana. Her car's parked along the road. Appears to have fallen down the embankment. Ended up at the edge of the river in the rocks."

"Have you called the coroner yet?" Cash asked.

"Raymond's on his way. He said he would stay at the scene and wait for you. We've got a semi overturned in the southbound lane between here and Gillette."

"Go ahead and respond. I'm on my way. You ID the body?" Cash asked. He hoped it wasn't a local. This was the part of his job he hated. Before the day was out, he could be banging on a door somewhere in the county to inform a relative that their loved one was dead. He also hoped it wasn't the missing Lenore Johnson.

"A woman. I'd say about sixty. The car is locked, keys in the ignition. Her purse is inside along with what looks like a half-empty fifth of vodka. I didn't attempt to open the car—did run the plates, though. The car is registered to an Emma Ingles."

Chapter Four

His head throbbing with pain, Brandon spent the better part of the day checking motels in and around the town of Sheridan, Wyoming, south of Antelope Flats, Montana.

Few of the clerks could recall a woman matching the description he gave. As luck would have it, he found where she'd been staying at the last motel he checked. Clearly, the woman he was chasing hadn't wanted to be found.

The Shady Rest Motor Inn wasn't an inn. It was barely a motel anymore. The place was on the old highway, too far off the Interstate to get much business other than overflow.

As Brandon walked into the office, though, he was delighted to see that he knew the clerk behind the desk. He'd met her at a party one of those times he'd come to Sheridan to get away and have some fun.

"Hannah, right?"

She grinned, obviously pleased he'd remembered.

They talked for a few minutes about everything but what he'd come for. When she mentioned that the motel owner had gone into town and wouldn't be back for a while, Brandon told her about the woman he'd been looking for.

"Yep, she was here. But she left before I came on this morning."

"I need to find her."

"You know I'm not supposed to do this," Hannah said.

"I wouldn't ask you, but it really is important," he told her. "She's in trouble and I'm trying to help her."

Hannah looked a little skeptical but called up the information on the computer. "She didn't check out, it looks like. She was registered as Anna Austin." Address? A post-office box in Richmond, Virginia. Virginia. That could account for the slight accent he'd picked up. No phone number. Nothing under a business.

"What's with you McCalls? Your brother called here this morning, too, looking for a woman," Hannah said.

"Cash?"

She nodded. "He was looking for another guest from Virginia. Lenore Johnson?"

The name didn't ring any bells. "They weren't in the same room, were they?"

Hannah shook her head. "They weren't even here at the same time." She shrugged. "Probably just a coincidence."

He rubbed his throbbing temples. Right now, there was only one woman he cared about. "Do you remember what Anna Austin was driving?"

"A black Ford pickup with Montana plates," Hannah said.

Why would the woman from last night have rented a pickup truck? She'd looked like a fancy-sedan kind of woman.

He thanked Hannah and left before her boss got back. The more he thought about the black pickup, the more sense it made. If you wanted to blend in in this part of the country, a pickup would be the way to do it. Especially if your mission was vandalizing coalbed methane wells on the VanHorn Ranch. A pickup wouldn't have raised suspicion like a car, if seen on the ranch.

The fact that she'd probably left the motel in the wee hours without checking out convinced him that she knew he would be looking for her. In fact, she probably figured all of the VanHorn ranch hands and the sheriff's department were searching for her, as well. She wouldn't know that he couldn't go to Mason VanHorn.

So she would try to find some place to hide. In this part of the country, that could be anywhere. Or she'd give up and leave.

His instincts told him she wouldn't give up. Not her.

He had the feeling that she hadn't gotten what she'd broken into the ranch house for last night. The safe had been empty by the time he'd come around. Completely empty. What thief took *everything* in the safe? A thief in a hurry. Or one who found nothing but bundles of money.

Except she hadn't had any kind of a bag with her. He would have seen it as skintight as that Lycra outfit had been. She hadn't planned on taking much with her.

He wondered what exactly she'd been looking for, then. Or if she was even a reporter. He didn't know any reporters who committed vandalism and breaking and entering for a story.

What he tried not to think about was how she'd hoodwinked him. She'd seemed so scared, so vulnerable, so caught. And all the time she'd just been playing him until she could get her hands on that lamp to throw at him.

She'd played him for a fool.

He drove back to Antelope Flats, tired, head aching, thinking only of a hot bath. He knew her name and what she was driving. He'd see her again. He was sure of it. Tonight.

One of the VanHorn Ranch pickups was just pulling out of the Longhorn Café. The ranch hand flagged him down.

"Red asked me to find you. He wants you to stop by the ranch to talk about surveillance tonight."

"Sure. Did something happen?" he asked, worried that the break-in had been discovered.

"Not that I know of. I think Red just wants to catch that damned vandal before the boss gets back."

That damned vandal, Brandon thought as he drove out of town again, headed for the Van-Horn Ranch.

If things went as he thought they would, he'd catch the vandal tonight. He tried not to think about turning Anna Austin over to VanHorn as he drove south to the ranch.

SHERIFF CASH MCCALL dug the sides of his boots into the steep hillside, sliding in the loose rocks. Below him, coroner Raymond Winters stood next to the river's edge, his hands in his pockets, his eyes averted from the body.

"A trucker saw her from the road and called it in to the Wyoming Highway Patrol," Winters said when Cash reached him. Winters was fiftysomething, a quiet, solemn man who, along with being coroner for Cash's county, owned Winters Funeral Home in Sheridan, Wyoming.

"Thanks for staying at the scene until I could get here," Cash said.

"No problem. She hasn't been in the water long," Winters said. "Twelve hours, tops."

"Cause of death?" Cash asked as he photographed the scene and the body of the overweight woman lying faceup in the water.

"At this point? I'd say a blow to the head."

"Any sign of a struggle?" Cash asked.

"Won't know for certain until I get her back to the lab, but you can see there is some bruising on the fleshy part of her upper arms."

"As if someone had grabbed her, maybe pushed her?"

Winters shrugged. "Women that age bruise easily."

"I heard her car is up the road, locked, keys in the ignition, a half-empty fifth of vodka lying on the floor."

Winters nodded. "I wouldn't be surprised to find her blood alcohol elevated."

Cash looked back up the steep embankment to the highway. "You think she fell?"

"Looks that way. Stopped to relieve herself

beside the road, locked the keys in her car, started walking home—she just lives up the road a couple of miles—got too close to the edge, slipped and fell. If she was drunk, it could explain it. She worked the night shift at Brookside and was probably coming from work."

"*Brookside?* I thought that place had been closed for years."

"The state took it over back in the eighties, closed the hospital, but has to have someone up there at night because of the darned kids until it sells," Winters said. "You know kids."

Cash nodded, remembering a night he and his brother Rourke went up there. An old haunted-looking huge building that sat dark and foreboding against the horizon about halfway between Antelope Flats, Montana, and Sheridan, Wyoming. The place scared the hell out of him, partly because of all the stories he'd heard about it. And partly because of the bad vibes he'd felt there that night.

He finished shooting the scene and put his camera away. "Next of kin?"

Winters shook his head. "Widowed. No kids. Lives alone."

"You knew her pretty well?" Cash asked.

"Not really. Just in passing." Winters rubbed the back of his neck. "Okay to go ahead and get her out of the water?"

Cash nodded. "A boyfriend?" he asked, thinking of the bruises.

Winters shook his head. "Highly doubt it."

"Problems with neighbors, work?" Cash asked, still worried about the bruises.

"None that I know of."

Cash glanced again up the embankment. He could see where she had fallen. There were indentations in the loose gravel and blood on the rocks along the river.

"Let me know when you have her blood alcohol levels." Cash figured he knew what would come back. Emma Ingles had drank too much, gotten out of her car for some reason and just lost her footing and fell, her body coming to rest in the water at the edge of the Tongue River.

But it nagged him that she would stop this close to home.

It was a sad end, but no reason to think of foul play. At least not at this point.

Still, Cash decided to put in a call to her boss at the former mental hospital and maybe her coworkers or neighbors. Wouldn't hurt while he waited for the autopsy report.

RED DIDN'T GET UP when Brandon walked into his office on the VanHorn Ranch. The first time he'd seen Red had been outside the Longhorn

Café. Red had approached him, having over-heard him say he needed another job if he hoped to go to law school on his own—which was the only way he was going.

Brandon wasn't asking his father for money. Because then Asa would ask him about the money he'd been left by his grandfather and he'd have to admit that he'd blown it all. No way.

That day on the sidewalk, he'd known the new VanHorn Ranch manager hadn't realized he shouldn't be hiring him. Red obviously either didn't know about the feud or didn't realize its magnitude.

Brandon wondered now if Red was wiser, if somehow Mason VanHorn had found out he had a McCall working for him. Or if Red just wanted to see him about security tonight like the ranch hand had said.

On the way into the VanHorn Ranch compound, Brandon had been relieved to see that Mason VanHorn's big expensive car hadn't been parked in front of the ranch house. Van-Horn was still in Gillette, so that meant he didn't know about the break-in, right?

The last thing Brandon wanted to do was run into the man, so he hoped to make this meeting with Red as short as possible. That's why working nights had been so ideal. No chance of seeing the big boss.

"Thanks for coming, Brandon. Sit down," Red said, and at once Brandon knew something was wrong. Before he could get seated, Red asked, "Run into any trouble last night?"

Was it possible someone had seen where the bathroom window had been pried open? Or had someone gone into the house and found the broken lamp in Mason's office?

Red pointed at the bandage on Brandon's head.

He'd forgotten about the injury and since he'd been taught to remove his hat when entering a room, he'd taken if off and now held it in his lap. "Accident after work. Wasn't paying attention. Took a fall."

Red nodded, measuring him, his gaze saying he knew Brandon was lying. "When I hired you, you didn't mention that your family doesn't get along with the VanHorns."

"I didn't think it was relevant," Brandon said truthfully. "I've never had anything against the VanHorns. It's just some old feud that no one seems to know how it got started. Is there a problem with my work?"

"Someone broke into the ranch house last night. Since it falls within your section of the ranch, I thought you might have seen something."

Brandon liked Red—would have liked to tell him the truth. But if he did, he could kiss off any chance of catching the woman. It wasn't just his pride. He owed her.

Before he could answer Red's question a side office door banged open.

Brandon turned, unable to hide his shock as Mason VanHorn stormed into the room. He was a big man, much like Brandon's father, Asa. But where Asa was blue-eyed and blond, Mason was dark.

Over the years, his once coal-black hair had gone from salt-and-pepper to white. Having seen Mason only in passing in town, Brandon couldn't hide his shock at how much Mason had aged—or the fact that he was here—and the ruse was up.

"He asked you why you didn't see this mysterious person who broke into my house," Mason shouted towering over him.

That wasn't exactly what Red had asked him, but Brandon didn't point that out. He could see that he was toast no matter what he said. Surprisingly, his first instinct was to tell the truth. But when he thought of Anna Austin, he knew he couldn't do that. He did his sheepish look. "I fell asleep."

"Like hell," Mason raged. "You were one of the vandals. Who was the other person?"

Brandon shook his head. "I didn't break into your house. I was guarding your wells."

Mason let out a curse that rattled the windows. "What the hell were you doing working on my ranch, anyway?"

"I need the money to go to law school," he said truthfully.

"Why wouldn't you just ask your father for the money? It isn't like Asa couldn't afford to send you to law school."

Brandon rose from his chair, refusing to let Mason VanHorn intimidate him. "It's something I wanted to do on my own, okay? I'm thirty-three. Isn't it possible I want to be my own man?"

"You should have been your own man when you were eighteen," Mason snapped.

Brandon smiled and nodded. "I guess I'm a late bloomer." He was eye-level with VanHorn, matched him in size and had youth on his side. And yet he felt a small tremor when he looked into the man's dark eyes.

If half the rumors about VanHorn were true, Brandon had every reason to be concerned he might never get off this ranch alive.

"You're spoiled rotten, like all the McCalls."

Brandon said nothing, seeing how this could escalate. Also, he *had* been spoiled. And wild. And foolish. And he should have grown up a long time ago.

Also, Mason was spoiling for a fight. "If I find out that's your blood in my house, that you vandalized my wells and broke into my house—"

"I'm not a vandal or a thief. Whatever the deal is between you and my father, it has nothing to do with me." He gingerly put his hat back on his head.

Red handed him his paycheck and he took it. Mason was still seething. "You're fired."

"I got that," he said, folding the check and putting it into his shirt pocket.

"So now you'll run to Cash the way you ran to Rourke when you lost money gambling with my last ranch manager," Mason said.

So Mason knew that his former ranch manager, Ace, had been fleecing not just the hired hands in the valley, but one of the McCalls.

Brandon felt his face heat. Not with anger but with embarrassment and shame. He'd lost a lot of money by being young and foolish. And now he knew that Mason VanHorn had known.

"I learned my lesson," Brandon said.

"An expensive lesson," VanHorn noted with no small satisfaction.

Brandon smiled. "It certainly was. I'm glad to see at least you enjoyed it. But you know, your former ranch foreman 'Ace' Kelly taught me an invaluable lesson about men who deal off the bottom of the deck. Whatever happened to him anyway? He rip off the wrong cowhand?"

Word in the county was that Kelly had just disappeared. A day later, Red Hudson had showed up and taken his place. Was it possible Kelly had gotten on Mason's bad side? Mason was famous for always getting even for the most minor of slights. Brandon couldn't help but wonder if Kelly wasn't buried somewhere on the ranch.

"I never want to see you on my property again," VanHorn said as if Brandon had hit a sore spot at just the mention of Kelly.

Brandon tipped his hat to Red, "Thanks for the job," and headed for the door, figuring he got off a lot easier than Kelly.

But now he had a major problem. How was he going to catch the woman? Worse, she had no idea about the trap she would be walking into with VanHorn back from Gillette.

Brandon had no choice. He'd have to sneak back onto the ranch tonight. He couldn't let her fall into VanHorn's clutches. Better to catch her and turn her over to his brother, the sheriff.

Only this time, if he got caught on the ranch, VanHorn could have him shot for trespassing. But what choice did he have? He knew what he was up against. No way did Anna Austin even have an inkling of how much trouble she was in.

ANNA CHANGED her clothing, putting on her swimsuit under a pair of shorts and a T-shirt. She packed a small backpack with the clothing she would need.

Her thoughts kept returning to Brandon Mc-Call. He'd been the only man who'd ever interested her. She shook her head, smiling at how foolish that sounded.

She'd only laid eyes on him one other time and he'd been years from being a man. But she'd fallen in love with him in an instant. Love at first sight. He'd stolen her heart. And since then, she'd measured every man she met against her idea of him—and they'd come up lacking.

He'd had the cutest, sweetest little grin she'd ever seen. She wondered if he still had it. Now at thirty-three, he'd grown into a heart-stopping handsome cowboy.

It had taken all of her control back at the ranch house last night to hide her surprise at seeing him again. Especially seeing him working for Mason VanHorn.

She'd always pictured him as her hero. So much for that fantasy.

As she walked past the phone on the table in the lake cabin, impulsively she picked it up and dialed the number she'd copied from Mason VanHorn's caller ID screen in his office. Dr. Niles French's number.

She held her breath as the phone rang four times, expecting any moment that she would hear his voice and lose control. An answering machine picked up. An automated voice said, "Dr. French is unavailable. Leave a message and he will return your call at his earliest convenience."

Hang up! The answering system beeped. Silence. She was breathing hard, fighting back tears. "I'm going to get you, you son of a bitch. I'm going to nail you and Mason VanHorn. Do you hear me? My name is Anna Austin and I'm coming after you with everything I have."

She slammed down the phone on a sob and was shaking so violently she had to steady herself against the table. She took deep breaths, trying to hold back tears of anger and frustration. She had to get control. She couldn't let Dr.

French and Mason VanHorn get away with what they'd done.

After a moment, her chest quit heaving, her pulse slowed and she straightened. She was still shaky. Knowing what Dr. French was capable of doing frightened her more than she wanted to admit. He was the boogeyman, the monster under the bed. He was her worst nightmare.

In the kitchen she filled a Baggie with sugar cubes, telling herself she shouldn't have called, shouldn't have warned him.

But she knew it was too late for that. She thought of the empty safe. Of the missing private investigator she'd hired. No, Dr. French knew she was after him. By now, Mason VanHorn did, too. But maybe she'd rattle them both and hope that one of them would lead her to the truth.

MASON HAD BEEN anticipating the call.

"I heard you had a break-in last night," Dr. Niles French said, sounding upset.

Mason swore under his breath, wondering who on the ranch had blabbed. He'd kill him. "It was nothing. A vandal protesting coalbed methane wells."

The doctor sighed. "You and I have known each other for how many years now?"

Mason didn't have time for a trip down memory lane. "What is it you want?"

"I want the records from the sanitarium."

Sanitarium. Mason almost laughed. It was a nuthouse. Loony bin. House of horrors. "What makes you think *I* have them?"

"Because I know you," Dr. French said. "Someone else has been looking for the records. I suppose you don't know anything about that, either."

"Why bring this up now?" Mason asked wondering if Dr. French had hired someone to break into his house for the file.

"I'm finished. I won't do anything else for you. I'm an old man. I'm not proud of things I've done. Especially concerning Helena and you. I would like to die in peace. I don't think that is too much to ask."

"You're not dying."

"Not yet. Mason, after everything I have done for you, grant me this last request. Give me my file. Let me destroy it. I just need to know it will never come out."

"Isn't my word good enough?"

The doctor sighed. "Let me be frank. I have less to lose than you do if anyone should ever find out."

"You aren't threatening me, are you, Niles?"

"Do you want me to come out to the ranch to get the file?" Dr. French asked. "Or do you want to come here?"

What Mason wanted was to tell him to go to hell, but he heard something in the elderly doctor's voice that warned him it would be a mistake. Why was it that when a person reached a certain age he felt the need to bare his soul? To make amends? To tie up loose ends? French didn't think there was a chance in hell that he was going anywhere after death that required a clear conscience, did he?

"I'll need a couple of days to get the file," Mason said. "I don't keep it here at the house."

"You aren't just stalling, are you, Mason?" Dr. French sounded old and tired.

Mason pitied him. "I wouldn't be that foolish. And you're right. It's never too late to end things."

"Yes. On that we can agree." Dr. French hung up.

Mason put down the phone. Hadn't he known this day would come? And yet he hated that it would have to end this way. Why couldn't they have both died peacefully in their sleep? Because neither had lived a peaceful life. Nor would there be any peace beyond this life. Not for the two of them.

Chapter Five

Brandon's only thought as drove north through Antelope Flats toward his family's ranch was of Anna Austin. He'd always loved the drive. The road climbed from Antelope Flats, giving him a view of the Tongue River Reservoir. The water glistened as the sun sunk in brilliant orange behind the Bighorn Mountains to the west. The red rock cliffs on the east side of the lake glowed golden just before he lost sight of the water as the highway curved away.

But today he only saw silken black hair, wide brown eyes and a face that would haunt him the rest of his days.

A few miles out, he slowed and turned onto the dirt road that followed Rosebud Creek through rocky outcroppings, thickets of chokecherry trees, willows and dogwood against a backdrop of sage and red rock bluffs and ponderosa pines.

Pulling up in front of the ranch house, he

looked up to see his little sister Dusty come out onto the porch as if she'd been waiting for him.

"What happened to your head?" she asked, smiling, making it clear she'd talked to her best friend Leticia. Dusty was all McCall, from her white-blond hair to her pale blue eyes and her need to know everything.

"As if you haven't already heard," he said, and stepped into the house.

She trailed right behind him. "Did you find her?"

"Who?" he asked, giving her his best innocent look.

"You can't fool me, Brandon McCall. You might as well tell me about her."

He shot her a smile over his shoulder as he trotted up the stairs to his room. "Don't hold your breath."

She was grumbling below him. His tomboy sister. She was almost nineteen but she still looked eleven to him. Maybe it was the way she dressed. Jeans, boots, western shirt, her hair pulled back in a braid, no makeup. Nothing girly about her. He felt a surge of love for her as he went into his room, closed the door and headed for the bath.

He showered and changed, dressing in the darkest clothing he had, then sneaked down the stairs, hoping to avoid the rest of his family if possible.

"You're not having dinner with us?" asked a female voice behind him.

He'd almost made it to the front door. Damn. He turned to look at Shelby, his mother. She was beautiful. He could imagine that she must have been stunning when she was younger.

"I'm going camping up in the mountains," he said.

She smiled at that, amusement in her gaze, and didn't ask about the bandage on his head. Obviously, she'd been talking to Dusty. "Maybe some time you could bring her out to meet your family."

The improbability of that made him smile. "Right. Yeah." He glanced at his watch. "I'm running late."

She nodded and waved him off. "Have fun." Yeah.

Things had been pretty weird at the house since his mother's return. Shelby Ward McCall had been dead to all of them for over thirty years. Then last summer, she'd just appeared at the front door as if returning from the grave.

Except she'd never been dead, no matter what the gravestone said at the local cemetery. Nope. Shelby and Asa had just cooked it up rather than get a divorce. At least that was their story and so far, they were sticking to it.

But Brandon, his brothers and sister hadn't missed that something was going on between their father and mother. Too much whispering, odd looks and times when one of them caught Shelby crying. Shelby wasn't one of those women who cried over nothing, which made them all worry that their parents had a secret between them that would make the others pale in comparison.

He tried not to think about it as he went to his pickup, got his shotgun and the supplies he'd purchased in town, and headed for the barn.

Saddling his horse, he loaded everything, including his sleeping bag, and swung up into the saddle, heading his horse south toward the Van-Horn Ranch. The sun was all the way down by the time he reached the first ridge. He stopped to look back on his family ranch, as he always did.

Like his brothers, there'd been a time when he'd tried to run from the ranching life, from the responsibility and the weight of a hundred-year-old tradition, mostly from the feeling that he had no choice in life but to follow in his father's and grandfather's footsteps.

Now, just the thought of leaving here to go to law school bothered him. What if for some reason—a job, money, a woman—he didn't make it back?

He shook his head at the thought and spurred his horse. It would be dark soon. He wanted to be on the VanHorn Ranch before then.

VanHorn would have all his men looking for Brandon McCall—and his pickup. The only way to sneak back on was by horseback.

He wondered how Anna Austin planned to get back on the ranch. It didn't matter. Whatever she pulled tonight, he'd be waiting for her.

MASON ANSWERED the phone. "What?"

"She called me."

"What? Are you drunk?" he demanded. "Look, Doc, I don't have time for this right now."

"Make time. Did you hear what I said? She called me and threatened me."

Mason was losing his patience. "Who are you talking about?"

"*Anna Austin.* Who the hell do you think?"

Mason felt all the air rush from his lungs. "That's not possible."

"She said she's in town and that she is coming after the two of us. I knew this was going to happen. I just knew it."

"She's not in town." Mason stumbled over to a chair and dropped into it.

"You swore this would never happen. I did everything you asked. You said that would be the end of it. Now do you understand why I wanted that damned file?"

His mind raced. "I'll take care of it. Do you hear me? I'll take care of it."

"Damn you for talking me into this," Dr. French said. "I want the file *now*. I'm not waiting a few days. You get it or else."

"Or else what?" Mason snapped. "Don't forget why you helped me. You needed the money or don't you remember?" he asked, his voice leaden with sarcasm.

"Yes," the doctor said. "I remember. But I'm too old to care now. All I have left is my reputation. I won't let you have that, too, Mason. You took everything else."

"Don't threaten me, Niles. Not if you know what is good for you."

"You can't control me anymore, Mason. If you don't give me the file, you will regret it." He hung up.

Mason slammed down the phone. "I already regret it," he said to the empty room. The old fool had to be mistaken. She didn't know anything about Dr. French. It wasn't possible. Nor could she be in town. He would have known.

Picking up the phone, he called Information for the number at the newspaper where she worked.

He was shocked to learn that she'd left that job six months before. The receptionist thought Anna Austin had resigned to do freelance investigative journalism. No, she didn't know of any other number she could be reached at.

If she had a cell phone, he had no way to get that number. His heart began to pound. He'd always feared that his secrets would get out someday. As he bent to pry up the floorboard and pulled out Helena VanHorn's worn dusty medical file, he prayed to God this wasn't the day.

ANNA TOOK back roads to the marina. She knew all the roads into the ranch would be watched, the house guarded. She had to get everyone away from the house and, at the same time, find a way to get in there herself.

She rented a boat for a week, even though she didn't expect to be in town that long, and left the truck parked in a stand of trees where she didn't think it would be noticed.

Once in the boat, she stuffed her gear under a seat. Then, powering up the motor, she eased away from the dock.

She'd had experience with boats because of the girls she'd met at expensive summer camps and even more expensive private schools. As soon as she was past the No-Wake buoys, she hit the throttle. The motor roared, the bow rising, then dropping as the boat picked up speed.

She couldn't help but smile as the wind and spray hit her face, blowing back her hair. She loved being on the water. There was nothing quite as freeing. She let the craft run full throttle, bouncing over waves from other boats, the sun in her face.

The Tongue River Reservoir stretched for miles from the steep red rock cliffs and pine trees to where the lake turned to river, flat and thick with brush and cottonwoods.

In places along the shore, she could see veins of black coal in the rocks. Up the river, there were coal mines that operated twenty-four hours a day. Sometimes she heard an occasional blast or caught sight of the huge crane at work.

It was getting dark. She watched the shoreline ahead, telling herself she had no choice other than what she was about to do.

IT WAS FULL DARK by the time Brandon stopped on a rise over the VanHorn Ranch complex. He scanned the buildings before him with night-vision binoculars. The ranch house was dark. Mason VanHorn's big car wasn't parked in front of the ranch house and he didn't see anyone guarding it, but he knew VanHorn and the others were there waiting.

And unless someone stopped her, Anna Austin was going to walk right into a trap. He thought about what he would do if he were her. She would have access to maps of the ranch. Several were posted on coalbed-methane-well Web sites. If she really was some famous investigative reporter, she would know where to look. He had to assume she knew the ranch probably better than he did.

She'd used vandalizing the wellheads as a distraction before, but she would know that none of VanHorn's men would fall for that again. It would have to be something bigger, something they couldn't ignore that wouldn't just draw them away from the ranch house, but force them away.

Tonight would be clear, with stars and a full moon. He was betting that she would make her move before the moon came up. And the moon would be up soon.

If he was right about her returning. His gut told him she'd be back. Or maybe he was just hoping. As he sat on his horse in the dark, Brandon smiled to himself at the thought of seeing her again. It was more than just his pride driving him, although he hated to admit that the woman intrigued the hell out of him.

Nothing moved in the darkness. He was beginning to think she'd outsmarted him again. Then he saw it. Down the mountainside, past the highway to Wyoming, past the ranch house. He focused the binoculars on what looked like a boat winding its way through the submerged trees where the creek drained into the lake below him. Hadn't he heard that VanHorn had purchased this narrow piece of swampy land?

"Anna," he breathed, and grinned.

She'd found a way back on the ranch.

Spurring his horse, he rode down the mountainside, following the cover along the creek. Clouds drifted over the tops of the large old cottonwoods as he headed for the lake—and Anna.

As he neared the lake's edge, he heard the *putt-putt* of a boat motor, then silence. Waves splashed at his horse's feet. He reined in and listened, hearing a soft metal thud, the lap of water and then stillness again.

Dismounting, he dropped his reins, leaving his horse to work his way to where he'd heard the last sound. The lake was up, many of the trees in this area now standing in water. He tried not to make a sound as he kept to the dense shadows of the trees.

A light splash, then another. Hunkering down at the base of one of the cottonwoods, he waited.

She came out of the water. Like last night, she wore all black, including the stocking cap covering her dark hair. Only tonight she had on all-black denim—and western boots. To his surprise, he realized she was dressed for horseback riding.

For a moment, he was too surprised to move.

She ran through the trees toward the fence line. An instant later, a half-dozen dark hulking shapes appeared out of the darkness. VanHorn's wild horses?

She didn't really think she could just climb on one and ride it, did she?

He stayed where he was, anxious to see what she planned to do, not wanting to spook her. It would do his pride good to see her lying on her back in the damp soft earth after being thrown—if she even got that far.

He watched her dig out something from her pocket. She was making a sound that had all the horses' ears up. She inched forward. A horse whinnied and stomped the ground.

Behind him, Brandon heard his own horse

whinny in answer. Several of the wild horses milled around, a couple shied a little, but came back to where Anna was standing.

He could only see her back, but she hadn't appeared to have heard his horse, didn't seem aware of him behind her, watching. Waiting.

To his amazement, the horses didn't run off as he'd expected they would. It was almost as if she'd been here earlier, the way they'd come up to the fence when they'd seen her. Almost as if they'd been waiting for her.

He saw her hold her hand out, palm down to one of the smaller of the horses. The mare nuzzled the closed hand. Anna didn't move a muscle. The mare nuzzled her hand again and slowly like a flower opening to the sun, the hand turned and opened.

Whatever she'd had in it quickly disappeared. She reached into her pocket for more as she began to stroke the horse's neck.

Brandon edged closer. He could hear her talking softly to the horse and the horse responding.

"Nice night for a boat ride," he whispered when he was within touching distance. He couldn't be sure VanHorn's men weren't within hearing distance. He wanted to save her—not throw her to the wolves.

She didn't even start, almost as if she'd known he was behind her. Either that or she had nerves of steel. The woman had grit, he'd give her that.

The horses shied, but didn't go far as she slowly turned to look at him. He was close, close enough in the darkness that he could see her face clearly, read her expression. No, he'd startled her, but she was hiding it well.

"Interested in a boat ride? I have a rental. You're welcome to go for a ride if you like," she whispered back.

He smiled at that. "I'm not really dressed for it. For that matter, neither are you. Planning to do a little horseback riding?"

She turned to the horses that had sneaked back over and dug what he realized were sugar cubes from her pocket. "They're beautiful, aren't they. I've always loved wild horses. They're built so different from domestic horses."

It surprised him. Not just her knowledge of horses, but her obvious love for them.

He leaned over to whisper in her ear. An errant lock of her dark hair tickled his nose. Her hair smelled of smoke, as if she'd been near a campfire. "I know what you're up to."

"Do you?" She didn't look at him as she

rubbed the mare between the eyes and dug out another sugar cube.

"Mason VanHorn came home today." He waited for a reaction, but didn't get one. "He's set a trap for you." For us, Brandon thought. "If you try to go back up to the ranch house, he'll be waiting for you."

"I see. And he sent you down here to tell me." She climbed up onto the fence, straddling it as she sat on the top rail.

"I'm trying to save you," he said and climbed up, as well.

"Oh, I thought your job was security—not protecting women who wander onto the ranch. You save a lot of women, do you?"

He watched her continue bonding with the mare. Several other horses stayed close, curious, but leery.

He knew the feeling as he looked at this woman. "You think VanHorn sent me?" That was so ludicrous it was laughable, but then she didn't know he'd been fired. Or that he was a McCall and shouldn't have been on this ranch to start with.

She raised a brow but said nothing.

The sky glowed golden over the mountains to the east of the lake, warning that the moon would be up soon. "You have to give this up.

Whatever it is, it isn't worth getting yourself shot over."

The night air was cool. His boots were wet from wading at the edge of the lake. He could see that her jeans and boots were wet, as well.

"How's your head?" she asked quietly without looking at him.

"Fine." A lie. It still ached. A constant reminder of her. As if he needed another one.

"Have you ever ridden a wild horse?" she whispered.

"One of these brought up from Wyoming's Bighorn?" He shook his head. "And I wouldn't suggest you try to ride one, either, if I were you. I know VanHorn's been breeding them and they might not be as wild as the others, but they sure as heck aren't broken, either."

The peal of a bell filled the night air, startling him. A dozen lights blinked on at the ranch complex. An engine cranked over. Then another. The bell continued to ring. The fire bell!

Anna swung her leg over the fence railing and slipped onto the mare's back as if she'd done it before, earlier. She was going to try to ride that wild horse bareback!

The thought was hardly formed when the horse took off running with Anna hunched over its neck, her fingers entwined in the mare's mane.

She was getting away.

Worse, she was headed in the direction of the ranch house. Headed right into an ambush.

Brandon leaped from the fence and raced back to where he'd ground tied his horse. Damn the woman! He'd tried to warn her. Didn't she realize that VanHorn would have told his men to shoot first and ask questions later? After all, this was Montana and trespassing could get you killed.

Swinging up into the saddle, he took off after her. As the first stars spread a pale glitter overhead, he and Anna streaked across the wide pasture to the thunder of hooves and the peal of the ranch bell. He was gaining on her, but only marginally.

That's when he saw it. A line of orange off the mountain from the ranch house, down not far from the water's edge. A grass fire!

He knew instantly what she'd done. The whiff of smoke he'd smelled in her hair. She'd started the fire as a diversion! VanHorn would go ballistic. What could be so important in that house that she'd get herself killed for it? Or, if she were lucky, only have to go to prison?

He could smell the smoke on the breeze as he raced across the nightscape. It was a smell every landowner in this part of the country feared. A grass fire could sweep across acres in a matter of minutes. There was nothing more dangerous.

Especially on a ranch with hundreds of coal-bed methane gas wells.

As he galloped after her, he could see movement at the ranch complex, men running, tanker trucks roaring off toward the blaze, other vehicles racing from the corners of the ranch as the alarm went out.

He was gaining on her, but she was almost to the ranch house. She'd headed for the back again and the shelter of the tall pines. Brandon could see the line of the fire flickering up in orange waves as the flames rode the light breeze. There weren't any wells for several miles from where she'd started the blaze, but if the breeze kicked up—

With a shock, he realized that he'd underestimated the lengths this woman would go to. Vandalism. Breaking and entering. Now arson? She was looking at some hard time—if Mason didn't get her first.

She rode straight for the ranch house, a deep shadow moving swiftly, her small form almost lost in the horse's silhouette.

One thing was clear. The woman could ride. He spurred his horse, knowing they both could be seen from the ranch house as the moon crested the mountain behind them. Mason VanHorn could have the crosshairs of his rifle on either of them right now.

The moon came up behind them, washing the ranch in shimmering gold. Anna disappeared into the tall pines. He was almost to the dark pines behind the ranch house when her horse came barreling out without her.

"Damn woman," he swore as he swung down from his still-racing horse. The moment his feet hit the ground he was moving. Right into whatever trap VanHorn had laid for them. He wasn't even sure a fire was going to do the trick this time. But he couldn't turn back. He couldn't let her fall into VanHorn's hands. The woman had no idea how dangerous that would be. He was sure she'd never dealt with a man like Mason VanHorn before.

It was pitch-black as he barreled into the stand of large pines, all moonlight extinguished under the wide dark sweeping branches. He didn't see her and sure as hell didn't see the tree limb she swung until it was too late.

She caught him in the chest. The limb wasn't very large. Fortunately for him, she hadn't had much time to find a good one.

All the limb did was knock the air out of him

for a few precious seconds. Not long enough for her to turn and run. He grabbed her, swinging her around to face him as he wrenched the limb from her and tossed it aside.

She jerked out of his grip and backed a few inches away from him, as if she knew he'd take her down if she ran. "I can't believe you work for someone like Mason VanHorn."

"*Worked.* He fired me this afternoon."

"I don't believe you," she whispered harshly.

"Fine. Then believe this. You don't have any idea who you're fooling with here. This man will kill you," he whispered back as he stepped a little closer. He could see that if he reached for her, she would fight him like a wildcat. But he wasn't letting her go near that house. "It's a trap," he whispered hoarsely. His chest ached. So did his head. He was getting tired of this woman hitting him. He could hear one of the fire trucks coming back up the hillside. Was it possible they'd already put the fire out? If so, the others would be coming, as well. "We have to leave *now.*"

"Not until I get what I came for," she said through gritted teeth.

"Didn't you just hear me? It's a trap. He's waiting for us inside the house."

"Wrong," said a deep male voice behind them. The night filled with the sound of a shotgun shell being slammed into its chamber. "I'm right here."

Chapter Six

Brandon froze at the sound of Mason Van-Horn's voice behind him. He started to turn, the ground muddy from last night's rain, but stopped as he felt the icy cold barrel of a shotgun press into the flesh behind his left ear.

"You've vandalized my wells, broke into my house and now you try to burn down my ranch?" VanHorn's voice rose with anger and contempt. "I should shoot you right now."

"I wouldn't suggest you do that," Anna said, stepping out of the dark shadow of the trees. Her voice sounded strange. Too calm for what was happening here.

The woman had no fear. No sense, either. Brandon looked at her, wondering what he'd gotten himself into. Moonlight filtered through the pines as the moon, huge and golden, cleared the mountains. He could see anger etched into her features. She should have been scared wit-less. What the hell was wrong with her?

He heard a sound behind him, almost a groan. Suddenly he didn't feel the cold steel of the shotgun. He turned, afraid VanHorn had pointed the gun on Anna. As he spun around, he saw VanHorn slip in the mud and start to fall, dropping the shotgun as he tried to break his fall.

Brandon grabbed the fallen shotgun and reached for Anna.

She stood staring down at the elderly man sprawled in the mud. VanHorn was trying to get to his feet.

"Come on!" Brandon gave her arm a jerk and she seemed to come out of the fog she'd been in. Grabbing her hand, half dragging her, they ran to his horse. He heaved VanHorn's shotgun into the darkness and swung up into the saddle, drawing her up behind him. "Hang on," he ordered, as if he needed to. Her arms were already wrapped around his waist as he spurred his horse and took off up the mountain-side. He could feel her shaking now as if in shock.

Behind him he heard the sound of voices. VanHorn's men must have found him. They would be hot on Brandon's trail. He rode hard for the next stand of trees. If he could reach forest-service land, he knew he could lose them. The terrain was steep and wooded. There was no way VanHorn could follow by pickup. And there was little chance of being tracked by horseback until daylight.

His horse lunged up the steep mountainside to where VanHorn land ended and forest-service land began. He'd left his gear at a spot high on the mountainside along a creek. He rode to it as the moon rose higher, making the night almost as bright as dawn.

Ahead, he spotted the old waterwheel, the blades wooden and weathered. Beside it a small shack. He reined in the horse and started to reach back to help Anna off. She slid off with ease on her own and walked toward the creek and waterwheel as if they hadn't been doing anything more tonight than going for a moonlight ride.

"Are you suicidal?" he demanded as he swung down and followed her. He'd bought himself a world of trouble and all because of a woman. One he would probably never understand.

The moon was high, casting a glow over her as he joined her. To his surprise, he saw that she'd been crying. Something softened inside him.

"Are you all right?" he asked, thumbing away a lone tear on her cheek.

She nodded and bit her lower lip as she looked again at the waterwheel. He'd put his pack at the opening to the shack. The small worn structure had no windows or even a door, but it was dry inside, the board weathered gray and soft from wear.

"This is your camp," she said, sounding surprised.

He could see now that she was trembling. She hadn't shown it, but she *had* been scared back there. He was relieved that the woman had a little sense.

"I'll get a fire going," he said. She didn't answer. He'd stacked some wood earlier while he'd waited for it to get dark. Now he went to the fire ring, and lighting a few tiny twigs, got a flame going. Carefully he added larger sticks until he had a good blaze, then put on some logs.

She hadn't moved, her back to him, as if she needed a few minutes alone. He gave them to her as he unsaddled his horse at the edge of the mountainside. Below him, he could see the valley, the Tongue River Reservoir a basin of liquid gold in the moonlight.

If VanHorn's men tried to follow them tonight, he would be able to see them coming.

Not that he anticipated that happening. No, VanHorn would wait until first light. If he came after them. Brandon was betting VanHorn would expect him to go home to the Sundown Ranch where he would feel safe.

Turning back to the fire, he saw that Anna was standing beside it warming her hands. The fire cracked and popped, sending sparks drifting up like fireflies.

"Why didn't you let me get caught back there?" she asked, staring into the flames as he joined her.

"What makes you think you *aren't* caught?"

She raised her eyes to him. All that honey-brown glistened in the firelight. "Why were you working for Mason VanHorn?"

"I needed the money."

"Badly enough to work for a man like that?" she asked.

"The job was temporary. Mason found out I was on the payroll and I got fired. It was bound to happen. The VanHorns and the McCalls have been feuding for years. I have no idea what started it and I don't care."

"If you were really fired, then what were you doing there tonight?"

He took off his Stetson and raked a hand through his hair. "I *was* fired."

She nodded slowly.

"I was there tonight because I wanted to try to keep you from riding into a trap. I had thought you might have the good sense to believe me. I was wrong."

"I'm sorry I misjudged you." She sounded as if she might mean it. "I just assumed that you were still working for Mason. Why would you take a chance like that otherwise?"

"I owed you." He turned where she could see the bandage on his head.

"Sorry. I didn't mean to hit you so hard."

"Uh-huh."

She closed her eyes in a grimace. "And I hit you with the limb, too."

"Uh-huh."

When she opened her eyes they were filled with tears. "I'm sorry I got you involved in this."

"That makes two of us, but it's a little late for that now," he said.

"Not if you give me your horse and let me go. When this is over, I'll make sure Mason Van-Horn knows you were never involved."

"When this is over?" He laughed. "No way are you going anywhere without me. I'm up to my neck in trouble *now* because of you, and you're going to get me out of it right away—

not when this is over. It's over now. In the morning, I'm taking you to the sheriff so you can turn yourself in. He's my brother. You tell him everything, clear me, confess to your crimes and if you haven't pulled these kinds of stunts before and gotten caught, the judge will probably give you probation."

"If I were to do that, you'd never convince Mason VanHorn that you weren't in on it with me," she said, shaking her head. "Isn't it clear to you that he has something to hide? Until I get the goods on him, neither of us will ever be safe."

"Why do I get the feeling you're about to make me another offer? Just so you know up front, I don't do business with vandals, burglars and arsonists."

She glanced toward the pack he'd left suspended in a tree. "Is there food in there?" She obviously knew there was. This was bear country. Any food had to be put up high enough to discourage the varmints from stealing it. "I'm starved."

He studied her. She was trying to change the subject, stalling. But he wasn't sure he was ready to hear her new offer anyway. Not that she could make him an offer he would accept, he told himself. "I brought some hot dogs."

Her expression brightened. "I can't remember the last time I roasted hot dogs over a fire. Do you have mustard, ketchup and relish?"

"What, no onions?" He laughed as he dragged up a stump for her to sit on. You would have thought he'd offered her a throne the way she smiled in gratitude.

He set about whittling two long sticks, handed her one and got the small insulated bag of food inside his pack down from the tree. He watched as she speared a hot dog on her stick, then carefully held it over the glowing fire, turning the hot dog slowly, the skin blistering and bubbling before turning perfectly brown.

Digging out the ketchup and relish fast-food packets, he handed them to her. "You almost look as if you'd done this before."

"Summer camp."

"Is that where you learned to ride?"

"I've always loved horses," she said. He wondered if she'd dodged his question on purpose. He'd never seen a woman ride like that. She'd obviously ridden more than just at summer camp.

She slid her hot dog off the stick directly into a bun. He watched her lather the dog with ketchup, then squeeze relish onto it. She took a big bite, closing her eyes as she chewed, making an "Mmm" sound.

He couldn't help but smile watching her. In the firelight she was adorable, the light sprinkling of freckles across her cheeks and nose as golden as her brown eyes. He reminded himself just who he was sharing his meal with.

She swallowed a bite and settled her gaze on him across the fire. "You can't turn me in."

He gave her a look that said he could and would. "What did you think was going to happen after everything you've done?"

"Trust me, I have my reasons," she said. "Help me and I promise you won't regret it."

"I *already* regret it."

"Please." The word came out a whisper.

"Save your breath," he said as he speared a hot dog and stuck it directly into the flames knowing it would burn on the outside. He didn't have the patience to cook his the way she did. He told himself he liked 'em burned.

She watched in horrified amusement as his hot dog caught fire, quickly changing her expression when he shot her a look. She'd taken off her black stocking cap and held it by the fingertips of one hand. Her dark hair tumbled in a cascade of loose curls, shiny black in the firelight, down around her shoulders.

She seemed smaller to him. Not the strong, determined woman he knew her to be. She rose and walked to the edge of the mountainside, her back to him. She seemed deep in thought, but he knew she could just as easily be plotting how to get away from him. There was no doubt that she wasn't finished with Mason VanHorn. Clearly the woman had a death wish.

He pulled his burnt hot dog from the fire and rested the stick against a rock. "You might as well make yourself at home. We're not going anywhere until daylight," he called to her.

She turned slowly and came back to warm her hands over the fire, her gaze on the fire, not him. "You don't understand."

"We can agree on that." He picked up the stick with the burnt hot dog, burning his fingers as he pulled off the wiener and dropped it into a bun.

"There are some papers I know he's hidden in the ranch house," she said. "I *have* to find them."

"Weren't they in the safe?" he asked, taking a bite of his hot dog.

She shook her head. "The safe was empty."

He chewed for a moment, watching her, then swallowed. "You just happened to have the combination."

"Men his age change the combination a lot and have to keep the numbers some place they can find them. I found them."

He took another bite before asking, "If these papers are that incriminating, why wouldn't he have already destroyed them?"

"He needs them if he wants to keep the others who were involved in line."

Brandon stared at her. *"Blackmail?"*

"Not exactly. Insurance."

"You seem to know him pretty well," Brandon commented after finishing his hot dog. "Is he blackmailing *you?*"

She shot him a disbelieving look. "You think I would be involved in something—" She waved a hand through the air in obvious frustration. "I told you. I'm an investigative reporter. This is what I do. Find out everything I can about a subject so I know where to look."

"For the dirt?" He hadn't meant to sound so negative about her career path.

"If there is dirt."

He nodded. "You think he knew you were coming after him and that's why the safe was empty?"

"He knew someone was," she said. "I hired a private investigator to look into the allegations."

"And?"

"And she's disappeared."

IT WAS LATE when Sheriff Cash McCall got back to his office. As he walked in he saw that the message light was flashing on his phone.

"Cash, it's Raymond Winters. Call me. I found something interesting during the autopsy."

Cash quickly dialed Winters's number. He answered on the second ring.

"I thought you'd like to know Emma Ingles was sober as a judge," Winters said without preamble. "She hadn't ingested any of the vodka. But you want to hear something odd? There was vodka in her lungs."

"How would vodka get into her lungs?" Cash asked.

The coroner chuckled. "Only one way that I can think of. Someone tried to make it look as if she'd been drunk when she fell into the river by pouring the vodka down her throat. But since she was already dead, it went into her lungs."

Cash swore. "She was murdered?"

"Sure looks that way unless you can figure out how she managed to get that much vodka in her lungs, then walk down the road and throw herself off the embankment, hit her head on a rock and fall into the river—without taking *any* water into her lungs."

"Thanks, Raymond, for letting me know."

"One more odd thing. I found another bruise. This one at the base of her neck. She was hit hard with something."

"You don't think it was during the fall in the river?"

"No."

Cash shook his head thinking about Emma Ingles lying face up in the river. "What killed her?"

"A blow to the back of the head. I'd say it was inflicted before she was thrown off the embankment."

"DISAPPEARED?" Brandon echoed.

Anna didn't answer and he saw that she was crying. Oh, hell. "Don't cry."

"I'm not crying!" she snapped, and sniffed.

Right.

She was crying harder now.

Oh, hell. Being raised by a cantankerous old man and three older brothers, he didn't have a clue what to do when it came to women. Well, at least not the crying part.

This was all Shelby's fault. His mother. If she had stayed around like she was supposed to…

He got up to go around the fire and put a tentative hand on Anna's shoulder. "It's going to be all right."

She shot him a look that told him that was the wrong thing to say since it was an obvious lie.

"Okay, it's not going to be all right." He put his arm all the way around her and she turned into his chest, burying her face in his jacket. "But it could be worse. VanHorn could have shot us both back there."

She wiped her tears with her sleeve, still crying but laughing, too, as she leaned back to look up at him. "You always see the silver lining in every cloud, don't you?"

Not always, but definitely right now with her in his arms. He held her closer, dropping his cheek to her hair. It still smelled a little like smoke, reminding him just what kind of woman she was. She encircled his waist with her arms and leaned into him as if, for right now at least, she needed someone to lean on.

He hated how good it felt to hold her. He wanted to wring her neck—not comfort her. This wasn't over. VanHorn had seen them. He would come after them.

Not that it mattered at this moment. Brandon remembered his reaction to her the first time he'd seen her. It was nothing compared to having her in his arms. He had the strangest feeling that he'd been here before with her. It made no sense.

Just like the feelings she evoked in him. Just his luck that the first woman who ever made him feel like this was wanted by not only the law but also by his family's sworn enemy.

He touched her long, dark silken hair and thought he felt a shock of electricity shoot through his fingertips. The scent of her wafted up, mixing with the smell of the campfire, the pines, the summer night.

He'd never felt more alive, as if everything was suddenly extra vibrant, the intensity of it making him feel light-headed.

She stepped back, looking a little embarrassed as she wiped tears from her cheeks.

He took a breath, watching her, wondering about her, knowing he needed to back off. It would be a mistake to get involved with this woman. *I'm already involved. Yeah? Not as much as you'd like to be.*

"You never told me what VanHorn did that warranted vandalism, burglary and arson," he reminded her—and himself. His voice sounded a little husky even to him.

"Do we have to talk about this now?"

"Before we go any further here, I'd like to know what I'm involved in." Brandon knew in all fairness that he'd involved himself. He could have radioed Red Hudson last night, let the ranch manager handle it. But he hadn't. And now he had only himself to blame.

"Right now he thinks I'm in cahoots with you," Brandon said. "And given that the Van-Horns have always hated the McCalls—"

"That silly feud?"

"Silly? We're talking bad blood for several generations between the families. This little incident is only going to fuel the fires. And I can tell you right now my family will be as angry as VanHorn. No good will come of this."

"I'm sorry but if you had just left me alone, you wouldn't have to be here now," she snapped.

"I was doing my job," he shot back, even though that wasn't quite the truth.

"If you had been doing your job, you would have turned me over to Mason VanHorn. You were working for him. You say you're not working for him, but how do I know he didn't send you to intercept me and find out how much I know? Or maybe to destroy what evidence I have."

Brandon shook his head in disgust. "I haven't lied to you. Don't you wish you could say the same."

"You're wrong," she protested.

He gave her a look, then stepped away from the fire to unroll his sleeping bag.

SHE COULD HAVE kicked herself. She knew he wasn't working for VanHorn. He'd rescued her tonight. Brandon McCall was one of the good guys. She couldn't be that wrong about the blond-haired boy who'd saved her when she was nine. So why was she pushing him away? To protect him? Or herself?

"What are you doing?" she asked.

"Going to sleep. It's late and I'm tired."

"I'm trying to be honest with you. I can't tell anyone until I have proof."

"Uh-huh." He took off his jacket, rolled it up for a pillow, then stripped off his shirt and started to unbutton his jeans. He was more handsome than she had ever imagined he would grow up to be. His back was tanned and muscular and just the sight of him dressed only in jeans and boots took her breath away. It was the first time she'd ever *ached* for a man.

"You might want to turn your head," he said, amusement in his voice as he noticed her staring at him.

She couldn't hide the emotions this man evoked in her, and didn't want to try. She'd dreamed about Brandon McCall since she was a girl. He'd been her fantasy man, one she had idealized in her imagination.

But not even her imagination had done Brandon McCall justice. "Sure you won't share your sleeping bag?" she asked, only half joking. She rubbed her arms, chilled by her own thoughts more than the weather. "It's already getting cold and I'm not use to this altitude."

His gaze locked with hers, burning through her. "I'm not going back to the VanHorn Ranch. Neither are you," he said. "I'm taking you to the sheriff in the morning and there is nothing you can say—or *do*—to change my mind."

He thought she was trying to seduce him? "Brandon, you aren't going to just go to sleep and leave me standing here?"

"Brandon?" He froze, his fingers on the buttons of jeans as he frowned at her. "I never told you my first name. And come to think of it, you never asked."

ANNA REALIZED her mistake the instant his name was out of her mouth.

He stepped toward her. He was shirtless now and she couldn't help but notice the broad expanse of his chest, the soft blond hair like down that disappeared into the space where he'd unhooked the top two buttons of his jeans.

"How long have you known my name?"

"Now look who's suspicious," she said, and saw that he would have an answer or else. "I

asked around." Only she'd done the asking when she was nine, some twenty-two years ago.

He stopped just inches from her. His skin was wonderfully browned from working on the ranch without his shirt, his shoulders muscled, his arms strong and well-shaped, just like his slim waist and hips, his long legs beneath the denim.

She recalled being in his arms and the feeling it had evoked.

"Why would you ask around about me?"

This time? "I was worried about you. I thought I might have hit you a little too hard. I called the clinic."

He shook his head. "There is no way they would give out any information on a patient. Try again."

"It doesn't matter how I found out your name, does it?"

"Yeah, it does," he said, stepping so close she could feel the heat radiating off his body. His masculine scent filled her. He let out a low chuckle as if he knew he had her cornered. The sound reverberated in her chest making her heart pound a little faster.

"Just once, I'd like to hear the truth from those lips," he said, his voice low and rough with emotion as he stared down at her mouth.

She licked her lips. "We met once before last night at the ranch."

He leaned closer. "Trust me, I would have remembered."

"You were just a boy. I was sitting on the curb eating a Popsicle on Main Street. Some older kids were giving me a hard time. You saved me from them." She saw his expression. "I guess you don't remember." She tried to hide her disappointment. She knew she was being foolish. Just because he'd made a lasting impression on her—

"How old were you?"

"Nine. You were eleven."

He shook his head.

"It's all right. It wasn't that big of a deal," she said, trying to hide her hurt.

A muscle bunched in his jaw. "Oh, I remember all right."

She smiled sadly. "Sure you do. Then you probably remember that I was eating a grape Popsicle."

"It wasn't grape. It was cherry. You said it was your favorite."

She felt her eyes burn with tears. "You *do* remember." She couldn't help the bubble of joy that rose in her. "I shared my Popsicle with you. You said cherry was your favorite, too."

He stepped back, jerking his hat from his head to rake a hand through his hair. His pale blue eyes were cold with anger. "I remember that little girl. And I remember her *name*. My God, *you're* Christianna VanHorn? Mason Van-Horn's daughter?"

Chapter Seven

Anna felt her heart stop at the look of horror in his eyes. He remembered all right. "Brandon—" She reached for him but he pulled free.

He stepped back from her as if she'd just told him she was the devil in disguise. "Whoa! You're Christianna VanHorn?"

At that moment, she would have gladly denied it. She hated the look of shock and revulsion in his face. "Now you know. Only I go by Anna Austin."

He shook his head, anger in his blue eyes.

"I didn't lie to you."

"No," he said sarcastically. "You've been honest with me from the get-go. It isn't bad enough that the VanHorns and the McCalls have hated each other for years? I get involved with you?"

"We're not exactly involved," she pointed out, surprised at her own anger.

"Why don't you go by Christianna VanHorn?" he asked. "I mean, that's who you really are."

"Would that make it easier for you?" Anna quickly turned away to hide the tears that that swam in her eyes. Earlier in his arms, she'd thought they'd both felt something. Obviously it was only because he hadn't known whom he was with.

He stepped around her until he was facing her. She could see that he was still angry. Still shocked as if she had purposely deceived him so he would help her. Hadn't she?

"Why?" he demanded. "Why would you go after your own *father?* Vandalize his gas wells? Break into your own house? Try to burn down the place? Why?"

"Brandon, it's complicated."

"I'm sure it's complicated. You still can't be honest with me, can you?" He turned and walked away from her.

"Brandon? Please."

He stopped, his back to her.

She felt tears burn her eyes again. She'd known he would be shocked when he found out who she was. But it was the look of disgust that was killing her. "I can explain," she said, and reached out to touch his arm.

He drew back as if her touch burned him and

shook his head as if warning her to keep her distance. "You should have told me."

"Brandon, this isn't about that stupid family feud, is it? That has nothing to do with you and me—"

"The hell it doesn't. Your father will send out a pack of dogs to hunt me down the moment he realizes I haven't gone to my brother. After last night, he'll think we were in this together."

"That's why we have to stick together, help each other." Her voice broke. This wasn't the way it was supposed to happen. She'd known that one day she would see Brandon McCall again. But not like this.

"I should have turned you over to your father," he said, pulling away from her.

"You couldn't do that," she said to his back.

"Oh, yeah?"

"I know you. I knew the kind of man you would grow up to be. You couldn't give me up to my father and you can't now, just as you had to help me when I was nine."

His broad shoulders slumped, his head dropped, then slowly he turned back around to her, his eyes full of sadness. "Do you have any idea what you've done here?"

"That's why I need your help."

CHRISSY. Mason still couldn't believe it. He'd struggled to his feet in the dim light of the pines to see her and Brandon McCall take off on a horse. Together.

Dr. French was right. But Chrissy wasn't just in town. She was on the ranch. She was after him. She knew.

His worst nightmare had just come true.

Even when Red and a few of the men had come running out to find him muddy and shaken, all he could do was stare after the two as they disappeared into the darkness.

He ignored offers of help as he stumbled into the house and poured himself a stiff drink. "Leave me alone," he barked. Red left with the other men, but Mason knew Red hadn't gone far.

Mason dropped into a chair, suddenly too weak to stand, and took a long swallow of his drink. It burned all the way down. Chrissy. Or Anna Austin, as she called herself for her newspaper and magazine articles.

The ramifications beat him like golf ball-size hail. Shaking, he set the drink on the table and dropped his face into his hands.

His life had been one mistake after another. The only gift he had was making money and now he had more of that than he would ever spend and it meant nothing. He had no one.

All these years he'd thought at least he had Christianna—as long as he kept her thousands of miles away, as long as she never got too close, never found out what demons drove him, consumed him.

But now he no longer even had that. He knew what she was after—and what extremes she would go to to get it. She'd set the ranch on fire! Vandalized his wells! Broken into the house that had been her home!

But that was nothing compared to her ultimate betrayal. She was in on this with a McCall.

BRANDON STARED at Anna in the glow from the campfire, remembering the little girl she'd been. Not so different.

That day on the curb, she'd been holding her own, even against five big kids. She hadn't really needed his help. But she did seem to now.

He hadn't known when he'd shared her cherry Popsicle that she was Mason VanHorn's daughter, Christianna. Would he have helped her if he'd known?

"Why the hell didn't you tell me you were Mason VanHorn's daughter right away?" he demanded, not letting himself think about the freckle-faced girl with the cherry Popsicle or the beautiful woman who'd wanted to share his bedroll.

"I haven't been his daughter for twenty-one years," she said. "He sent me away."

Brandon didn't want to react to the pain he heard in her voice. He thought of his own mother. Gone for over thirty years. But at least he'd had a father. Anna hadn't had either all these years.

He looked at her, his emotions at war. "I can't believe you're Christianna VanHorn."

"Stop saying that like I'm the spawn of the devil. Even if it might be true."

He shook his head. Hell's bells, what had he gotten himself into this time? And more to the point, what had *she?* "You've lied to me from the start, beginning with your name."

"That's not true. Anna is my nickname. Austin is my middle name and my mother's maiden name. It's the name I write under. I never liked Christianna. It was so…"

"Long?"

She rolled her eyes. "Yes, long. Anna's the name my mother called me. She never liked Christianna. It had been my father's baby sister's name, a sister who had died when she was an infant."

He could only stare at her—all of it too much to comprehend. "*Why?* I still don't understand why you would go after your own *father?*"

"Believe me, I have my reasons."

The anger in her voice cooled some of his own. "But he's your *father*," he whispered.

"I told you, he hasn't been a father to me since I was ten. He put me in one boarding school after another, never letting me return to the ranch that I loved, keeping me at arm's length."

"Why did he do that?" He'd always heard that Mason idolized his daughter.

"Isn't it obvious? He was afraid that some day I would find out what a monster he really was. You have no idea what he is capable of," she said, her voice breaking with emotion. "I do."

MASON HEARD Red come back into the house and lifted his head from his hands, pulling himself together.

"Are you all right, boss?" Red asked.

"It was McCall. He's the one behind all of this."

"Brandon McCall?" Red didn't believe it.

Mason could see it in his face and he knew that if he lied to Red now, he would lose him. He needed Red. Needed someone he could trust. Especially now.

"There was another rider with him," Mason said. "A woman. I want McCall found and brought to me. Make sure the woman isn't harmed. And I don't want anyone to know about this, you understand? *No one.*" From Red's disapproving look, Mason knew he understood only too well.

"I'm not going to harm them, if that's what you're worried about."

"Why not call the sheriff and let him handle it?"

Mason gave Red a piercing look. "The sheriff," he said through gritted teeth, "is Brandon's brother. You think I can get any justice in this town? No sheriff. I'll handle this myself. Just like I always handle things." He could see Red wasn't going to move until he got the whole story. He sighed. "The woman is my daughter."

Red didn't hide his surprise. Or his sympathy. "She's the one who vandalized the wells, broke into the house and probably started the grass fire. Not McCall."

Mason swore. "What the hell is he doing with my daughter if he's not in on it?"

Red shook his head. "I've gotten to know McCall in the weeks he's worked for me. He didn't have anything to do with what is happening here. You fired one of my best men. If this is about that stupid feud—"

"I don't want him with my daughter," Mason snapped, remembering the day he'd caught his nine-year-old sitting on the curb sharing her Popsicle with the youngest McCall. They'd just been kids visiting on a hot summer day, but he'd had a horrible premonition when he'd seen them together. It was so strong he'd known he had to get his daughter away from Antelope Flats, away from Montana.

And now Christianna was back—and with McCall.

"I need to talk to her. Without him there," Mason amended. "You can understand that, can't you?"

"I can find them," Red said slowly.

"I thought you probably could."

"You want me to start tonight?"

"No, wait until first light when you can track them. I would imagine McCall will head to his ranch. If that's what he does, we'll wait until he leaves it again. We need to get him alone. I'll take care of my daughter."

Red seemed to hesitate, but then slowly nodded.

Mason waited until he heard Red leave before he reached for the phone and dialed Dr. French's number.

ANNA STEPPED AWAY from the fire to the edge of the mountainside again. A cool breeze came up out of the pines and the valley. Lights sparkled in the distance.

The only sound was the crackle of the fire and the gurgle of the creek through the rocks and the broken blades of the waterwheel. She breathed in the sweet smell of pine and the night.

"I don't want to talk about my father," she said without turning around. "Please."

She felt rather than heard him come up behind her. Suddenly the night was much warmer, her skin alive with just the thought of his touch.

"I'm sorry," he whispered, his breath feathering the hair at her right ear.

She closed her eyes, anticipating the feel of him.

His arms came around her, his fingertips making a torturous sensuous trail down her bare arms. He entwined his fingers with hers, drawing her hands back under her breasts as he hugged her to him. She leaned against his solid body and told herself not to trust her feelings—let alone fall for Brandon McCall. She'd seen the way he reacted when he found out who she was.

Yet as he turned her slowly around to face him, her eyes locking with his, she wanted with all her heart to believe in him. To surrender to her feelings. All breath left her as he bent down to brush his mouth over hers. Her lips parted on a sigh. His eyes were the palest blue she'd ever seen. In the moonlight they were like hot flames burning pure. She tried to catch her breath, to hear his whispered words over the pounding of her pulse.

"Anna." He said her name like a caress.

Her skin rippled with goose bumps, her heart galloped as wild as the horse she'd ridden earlier as she'd tried to escape this man. But she'd never been able to escape him, not in her thoughts, not earlier tonight.

And there was no escaping him now.

He lowered his head again and kissed her.

BRANDON DIDN'T WANT to react to the pain he'd heard in her voice. He thought of his own mother. Gone for over thirty years. Did anyone get over that feeling of rejection?

He drew her close, holding her. He wanted her, wanted Christianna VanHorn. Even as he thought it, he knew they had no future. The fact that she was a criminal aside, she was a *Van-Horn*. He was a McCall.

And still he kissed her, not surprised by the desire that flared inside him. Or the connection he felt to her, one that had begun with a cherry Popsicle years ago.

He didn't question the bond between them, nor the way she responded to his kiss, her lips parting as a sigh escaped her slim pale throat. He deepened the kiss, wanting her like nothing he'd ever wanted before. Passion sparked between them, like two powerful chemicals that should never be mixed. Not unless you wanted one hell of an explosion.

He pulled back, knowing the inevitable outcome if he continued kissing her and what those actions could cost them.

Moonlight filled her black hair with silver. Firelight danced in her brown eyes with flashes of gold. He looked into those eyes and what he saw there almost dropped him to his knees. A combustible mixture of desire and need.

"I've wanted to do that since I saw you last night," he said, his voice low and rough with emotion as he stared down at her mouth.

Anna pressed her fingers to her lips, her eyes bright with tears. He could see that she was shaken by the kiss. As much as he was.

He nodded and tried to still his raging heart. "You can have the bedroll. I'll be fine by the fire."

She smiled, tears in her eyes. "I'll go to your brother the sheriff with you in the morning if that's what you want. I'll fix things with my father for you. He won't press charges."

He stared at her. She would go to her father for him? "No, we're in this together now." Whatever the hell it was. "I'll help you."

Tears spilled down her cheeks. She swiped at them, biting at her lower lip as she looked at him. That look could have been his undoing if he touched her now.

But he didn't reach for her. Couldn't. He turned and picked up his shirt, drawing it on without looking at her. He pulled on his jacket, buttoned up his jeans and finally turned to find her still standing in the same spot.

She looked small and vulnerable and his first instinct was to pull her to him again, to hold her, comfort her, make love to her beside the fire. Just the thought of her naked in his arms made him groan.

He turned and headed off into the trees to find some limbs to keep the fire going tonight. Mostly he needed to get away from her for a while.

The fire had burned down to glowing coals by the time he returned. She was tucked into the sleeping bag, lying on her back as if staring up at the stars through the tops of the pines. Smoke curled up from the campfire. Beyond the glow of the coals was nothing but darkness.

"Good night," she said, not looking at him.

He pulled the log stump closer to the fire and stretched out, his back against it. "Good night…Christianna." He watched her close her eyes, her chest rising and falling beneath the thin bedroll. A single tear rolled down the side of her face.

It was going to be a long night.

Chapter Eight

Brandon woke to find Anna gone. He sat up, looking first toward his saddle. It was still where he'd left it, but he'd seen her ride bareback. Half-afraid, he glanced in the direction of where his horse should have been, almost surprised the mare was still there. Would Anna have taken off on foot? She could be miles from here by now.

Something splashed in the nearby stream. The day was just breaking through the pines. Van-Horn would have his men out looking for them.

Through the trees he spotted movement and the pink glow of bare skin. Another splash. She was taking a bath in an eddy in the creek.

He turned away, smiling to himself. Anna Austin was one of a kind. He quickly reminded himself that she was Christianna VanHorn—no matter what she called herself—or what he'd come to think of her as.

He'd promised her last night that he would

help her. That meant trying to find out what had happened to the private investigator she'd hired.

They would have to get moving soon, he thought as he busied himself with breaking camp. VanHorn's men would be after them. No way was VanHorn going to let a McCall get away with running off with his daughter.

But Brandon did wonder what VanHorn would do to Anna.

Now last night made sense—VanHorn slipping in the mud, dropping his shotgun. He'd seen his daughter. He must have been shocked to realize she was the vandal. And to see her with a McCall… VanHorn must be beside himself.

What had happened to make him push his daughter away? Something.

Was that what Anna was trying so desperately to find?

As he finished rolling up his bedroll and stuffing everything else into his pack, he heard her come up from the creek. He promised himself he wouldn't forget who she was. Not again. He would keep his distance. The last thing he wanted was to get more involved with her.

And last night he'd come close. He'd wanted to make love to her. No big surprise there.

No, what worried him was that she seemed to have a hold on him he couldn't explain—and had since the first time he'd seen her on the curb when he was eleven. It was her smile. The girl had been a heart-stealer. The woman…well, she was a heartbreaker.

He turned to look at her and felt all his resolve wash away. Her wet hair trailed down her back in a single braid. She looked all of sixteen with her hair like that, her face flushed from the cold water, her eyes bright.

He looked into her honey-brown gaze and found himself falling. It felt like jumping off a cliff without knowing or caring if there was water below you deep enough that you wouldn't kill yourself.

"Good morning," she said, all business. "Have you changed your mind?"

He shook his head, even though he wasn't sure what it was he was supposed to have changed his mind about. "Good morning, Anna." He couldn't bring himself to think of her as Christianna after he'd seen how much he'd hurt her last night when he'd called her that. "Changed my mind? You mean about helping you? No."

She cocked her head at him. "Is there something else you haven't changed your mind about?" She nodded knowingly. "About the two of us. Frightening, isn't it, just the thought of a VanHorn and a McCall."

She was making fun of him.

"Joke if you want, but can you imagine your father's face if you told him you were interested in a McCall?"

"As a matter of fact, I can. I saw his look when he came upon the two of us on that curb all those years ago," she said and smiled. "I'm not afraid of my father."

"Maybe you should be," he said.

Her smile faded. "Maybe I *should* be." She shivered and he opened his arms, not surprised when she stepped into them.

The bare skin on her arms felt like ice, but soon warmed as he drew her closer, holding her. After last night he couldn't turn her over to the sheriff any more than he could take her—and the trouble they were in—back to the ranch.

He didn't know what to do with her. She wasn't just a criminal, she was a *VanHorn*. He was a McCall. And as much as she wanted to believe that didn't matter, it did.

And yet when she pulled back to look up into his face, he kissed her, not surprised by the desire that flared between them. Or the feeling that he was powerless to prevent it.

He felt the heat of desire rush through his veins—shoving aside rational thought.

She drew back, cocking her head as if to listen, then smiled up at him, leaning against him to kiss him. She had the most wonderful mouth. He lost himself in her mouth, in the taste of her, in the feel of her skin beneath his fingertips as he cupped her face in his hands. He could have kissed this woman the rest of his life.

Suddenly she pulled back, her eyes wide, her breath coming quickly. "I heard something," she whispered.

He listened. He didn't hear anything. Except for the thunder of his pulse in his ears.

Then he did hear it. The sound of a truck engine coming up one of the logging roads below them.

CASH COULDN'T REACH Realtor Frank Yarrow until the next morning.

"Yes, Sheriff, what can I do for you?" the elderly Realtor asked.

"I'm calling about an employee of yours, Emma Ingles. She was a security guard at Brookside?"

"Oh, Emma." Yarrow sighed. "I heard what happened to her. What an unfortunate accident."

"I was wondering if there had been any trouble at Brookside recently."

"Trouble?"

Cash thought he heard something in the man's tone. "Did something happen up there?"

"No. This has nothing to do with Emma. It's just that I went up there the day Emma died to show the place to a woman. She'd been insistent on the phone, so I'd agreed to meet her there. She never showed. It's silly. I can't see that it would have anything to do with Emma. Unless the woman might have gone up there later that night."

"What was this woman's name?" Cash asked.

"I suppose I could give it to you," Yarrow said. "She had a Southern accent. I got the impression she wasn't really interested in buying the place, just curious. I'm afraid I get a lot of those." He chuckled. "When I heard about Emma it got me wondering if she could have gone up there last night, while Emma was working. Silly. It's just that Emma wasn't a drinker. Maybe this woman upset her. Or scared her."

"Her name?"

"Oh, sorry. I do get carried away sometimes. Lenore Johnson. At least that's the name she gave me."

Lenore Johnson. The missing private investigator from Virginia. Why had she wanted to see Brookside?

"We don't need any bad publicity associated to Brookside," Yarrow said, clearing his throat. "I'm having enough trouble finding a buyer for it."

"Then I'm sorry to give you some bad news." Yarrow would read about it in the evening paper anyway. "Emma Ingles's death is being investigated as a homicide."

"Oh, no. If it generates the kind of publicity it did the last time…"

"The *last* time?" Cash asked.

"The last murder. The one that ended up closing the place down for good."

"There was a murder at Brookside?"

"I can't remember all the details. You'd have to ask Abe. Abe Carmichael. He was the sheriff then. Some woman was killed in her bed up there. Pretty gruesome. They never caught the killer. Everyone just thought it had to be one of the other patients, you know? But after that, the place went bankrupt and the state took over the building."

Cash tried to remember when the institution had closed. He must have been about fifteen.

"Isn't it awful, but I can't remember the woman's name. Just the poor soul's room number. 9B. Was a grisly death. The killer never caught."

MASON VANHORN woke with a start, and for a moment he convinced himself that last night had been nothing more than a bad dream. Chrissy was in Virginia. She hadn't come to Montana without telling him. She hadn't vandalized his wells, broken into the ranch house or set fire to one of his hay fields. Not Chrissy, his precious daughter.

Not the cute, little sweet cheerful girl he'd known.

But he didn't know Anna Austin, the woman she'd grown into. The woman he hadn't even seen in more years than he wanted to admit.

He'd told himself it was better that way. Better for her to make a life for herself somewhere else. He'd done her a favor, whether she realized it or not.

He padded into the kitchen in his pajamas and made himself a cup of coffee. His hands were shaking as he lifted the cup to his mouth.

"You stupid fool." Dr. Niles French's words echoed in his head. "She's the one who hired that private investigator. She *knows*."

"She just thinks she knows," Mason had assured him last night on the phone. "You just do your part and let me handle her. And make sure you don't breathe a word about this. I don't have to tell you what could happen if you do."

He thought he'd already handled her. When Chrissy had called last week and asked about her mother, he'd just repeated the lie he'd told her since she was a child. A horrible lie, but much better than the truth.

He'd wondered then why she would be asking about her mother now, after all these years, but he hadn't let it concern him. He was so sure that she'd believed the lie. Just as she always had.

But now he knew differently. She had been the one who'd hired the private investigator. And now this. The vandalized wells, the break-in at the house, the fire she'd set. All planned with one thing in mind. To get her father. She'd come after him as if—

He sloshed the coffee in his cup onto the counter as it hit him. She'd come after him as if she already knew the truth. As if someone had told her.

He put down the cup and dropped his head. Suddenly, he felt very old and tired. And afraid.

She had no idea how dangerous this was. She would have to be stopped. As powerful as he was, he couldn't protect her. Not if she continued to dig into the past.

As THE SOUND of the truck grew closer, Brandon moved quickly. He saddled his horse and slipped to the edge of the ridge, staying in the trees to hide his movements. A stock truck with the VanHorn Ranch logo on the side and two horses in the back. They had tracked him this far already.

Brandon swore and turned to find Anna right beside him. They had only one choice. They'd have to run, and that meant deeper into the Bighorn Mountains, though. Two men could move faster on two horses than he and Anna could riding double on one.

He glanced toward the snowcapped mountains as he heard a horse whinny on the mountain below them, followed by the sound of the horses being unloaded. They had to move, and fast.

Anna shook her head as if seeing what he had in mind. "We need to double back," she said quietly. "The boat is hidden in the trees and I have a rented cabin on the other side of the lake."

"There's no way we can get past them, especially riding double, and they may have already found the boat."

"Trust me, they won't expect us to come back through the ranch. Why else would they have sent men up here? But you're right. I *do* need a horse. Fortunately, I know where I can find one." She cocked her head toward the horses now being unloaded from the truck below them on the mountain.

"What?"

"You distract them." She gave him a quick kiss on the cheek. "They'll never expect you to ride right at them. Give me a few minutes. When you hear this—" she sounded a bird call "—then come a-ridin'."

She didn't give him a chance to argue. She took off running through the trees. He swore as he hurriedly tied his pack onto his horse and swung up into the saddle.

The woman was going to get them both killed.

Brandon heard the clear call of the bird below him on the mountainside and the sound of the men unloading their saddles and gear. He just hoped they would be busy enough that they couldn't get to their sidearms.

He spurred the horse, riding over the lip of the ridge and dropping straight down toward the truck.

The men looked up at the sound. Anna was right about that much. They were surprised. And distracted. Brandon recognized one of them, a tall, skinny guy called Stick. Stick dove for the cab of the pickup, either ducking for cover or going for a weapon.

The larger of the two seemed nailed to the ground as Brandon barreled down on him.

The two had the horses tied at the back of the stock truck. One horse had a saddle on but not cinched down yet.

Both horses shied. The big man dove out of the way as Brandon shot past. Riding hard and fast, Brandon kept low in the saddle, fearing he'd wouldn't hear the report of the rifle until he'd already felt the bullet.

The road curved not a hundred yards past the truck. He rounded the corner and dropped off into the creek bed, reining in behind a stand of pines so he had a partial view of the road above him.

He hadn't been there a minute when he heard the sound of horses' hooves headed his way. He stayed where he was until he saw a flash of long dark hair blowing back from the small rider curved into the horse's body as if the two were one.

He couldn't help but smile as he spurred his horse and rode off after her. Behind them, he could hear the truck engine crank over. Anna must have heard it, too.

She dropped down into the creek, then up the other side, riding toward the lake in the distance, leaving the road behind as she took to the lightly forested hillside along the creek bottom. Over a few hills they lost sight of the road—and VanHorn's men.

When he caught up to her, she was grinning, her face flushed with excitement, eyes bright.

"That was one fool thing to do back there," he said. "You could have been killed."

"I could say the same of you," she said, still grinning.

He'd just bought himself more trouble and all for a woman he'd never understand. He was either crazy or... He shook off even the thought as he looked over at her.

Whatever this chemistry was between them, they had a snowball's chance in hell of taking it any further, even if she didn't live in Virginia and him in Montana.

"You're wrong," she said.

He looked over at her. "About what?"

"Us." She smiled. "There's something there, even you can't deny it."

"I'm not denying it. I'm just telling you it would never work," he said as he rode along beside her. "Hell, I don't even know why our families hate each other, do you?" He glanced in her direction when she didn't answer. "You *know?*"

"My father and yours fell in love with the same woman." She rode ahead of him and he had to spur his horse to catch up.

"What woman?" he asked, hearing the fear in his voice.

She didn't answer. He reached over and reined in her horse along with his. "What woman?" he demanded, wishing to hell he'd never brought this up.

Anna sighed, no doubt wishing she hadn't said anything. "Your mother."

He felt as if she'd hit him again, only this time with a baseball bat. "Shelby?" Oh, hell.

"Shelby Ward, now McCall."

All he could do was shake his head. "How do you know this?"

"Before I left for boarding school I found some letters your mother had written my father."

His heart dropped to the pit of his stomach. "When were they…involved?" His mother had supposedly died when he was about three.

"In high school."

He couldn't hide his relief as he let go of her reins and they started through a stand of tall pines, the air cool and moist, sunlight sifting down through the dark green boughs.

"You thought it was more recent?" she asked.

He hated to admit it.

"I heard that your mother…died for a while."

He'd never heard anyone put it quite like that. For some reason it struck him as funny. Or maybe he was just so relieved. "Sorry," he said laughing, "It's just… So we're talking fifteen, sixteen?" His relief made him feel buoyant. "Then it wasn't serious. Asa and Mason were both kids."

"You don't think you can fall in love when you're young?" she asked, an edge to her voice.

"Puppy love, maybe, but not real get-married-have-kids love. Not at that age." He caught her expression. "What?"

She took off on the horse and he had to gallop to catch her. He turned her horse, slowing them both.

"What did I say?" Had he hurt her feelings? "I'm sorry. Did you fall in love when you were a kid or something?"

"Or something," she said, shooting him a look that said he'd put his boot in it.

"I'm sorry." He reached out to touch her face. She was all soft and vulnerable again and all he wanted to do was kiss her. "*Asa* might have won Shelby, but he couldn't live with her. That's why they've been apart for thirty years. Except for that one moment of weakness when they conceived my sister Dusty," he said, trying to correct whatever he'd said that had caused the change in her.

"It's a stupid feud," she said after a moment. "If Shelby hadn't married Asa, then you wouldn't be here. The same for me if my parents hadn't gotten together."

He heard something in her tone, something he didn't think had anything to do with him or the feud. "I guess it was destined that we be born, huh?"

But it still didn't change anything between them. He tried to imagine what his family would say if he brought home Christianna Van-Horn—and quickly pushed the thought away.

Anna grew quiet as they followed a gully down to the lake and followed it as far as the edge of forest-service property. Brandon figured it was best not to say anything. He left his horse where his brother Rourke could pick it up when he called him. Rourke would do it without asking as many questions as either J.T. or Cash.

The boat was right where she said it would be. She slid off the horse she'd just stolen, letting it go on VanHorn property.

Brandon added horse theft to her other crimes as he followed her through the thick cottonwoods toward the water and the boat she'd left tied up there.

He'd half expected VanHorn and his men to be waiting by the boat—if they hadn't sunk it or set it adrift.

But the boat was where she'd left it. It seemed she'd been right about that, too.

She untied the boat and waited for him to get in. He could see other boats out on the water, fishing boats, bobbing along in the light breeze.

He climbed in and she pushed them out. At the back of the boat, he got the twenty-five-horsepower motor going. It putted softly as he backed out. He nosed the boat through the shallow water and trees toward open water.

"Where to?" he asked when they were out in the middle of the lake, out of sight of the Van-Horn Ranch. Water lapped at the metal sides of the boat, the sun beat down, the air was cool and scented with pine and water.

ANNA LOOKED INTO his face and couldn't help but smile as she pointed the way. There was something so genuine about his expression, his blond hair slightly curled beneath his Stetson, his blue eyes as intense as the sky overhead.

He'd been adorable at eleven. At thirty-three, he was ruggedly handsome. All cowboy. All man. Her body's reaction attested to that.

But their connection was more than physical. She'd felt it that day on the curb. She could still taste the sticky cold imitation-cherry flavoring and remember that strange feeling as if she could see into the future.

"At the cabin I'll tell you everything," she said impulsively.

He met her gaze. She could see the doubt, but he nodded.

She leaned back, closed her eyes and let the breeze blow her hair. The sun felt wonderful on her face. She didn't think about anything but this moment, here with Brandon McCall. After all these years of wondering what had happened to him, here she was—risking his life.

She opened her eyes as the boat slowed and looked at him, praying she was doing the right thing. Once she told him everything, there would be no turning back. He would know too much.

But Brandon was right. He was already involved. She'd thought she could protect him by keeping what she knew from him. She saw now that it was impossible. If she hoped to protect him, he had to know everything she did. Her father had seen them both last night. Seen them together. What would he do now? She hated to think.

Brandon glided the boat into the dock. He watched Anna jump out to tie it up, then joined her for the climb up to the cabin.

The sun burned down on them, the lake aglitter with the bright light. Behind them, boats roared past making large cresting waves, dogs barked in the distance and children splashed at the edge of the water in front of the rows of cabins.

Anna led the way up the stairs from the beach to the cabin perched on the side of the mountain. It was the farthest from the water, tucked back in the pines, but the view was spectacular.

Inside, there were two bedrooms with a stack of bunks in one, a double bed in the other. The kitchen was tiny, but the living room was large with wide windows, much like his family cabin across the bay.

Anna went straight for the table in the kitchen. As she turned, he saw that she held a worn manila envelope in one hand.

He saw indecision in her expression and held his breath, sensing that this moment was crucial for more reasons than he could yet understand.

"Maybe you'd better sit down," she said quietly.

He nodded and pulled up a chair. Was it possible she really was going to trust him?

"I received a letter a little over a week ago," she began. "It had been mailed nine years ago, but had been lost. It was from my former nanny, Sarah Gilcrest. In the letter, Sarah confessed to what she'd witnessed one night when I was three. My mother had been seven months pregnant. The doctor had insisted she stay in bed throughout most of the pregnancy. Late that night, she gave birth early."

Anna stopped, her fingers on the envelope quaking.

"You don't have to do this," he said, seeing how hard this was for her.

"Yes. Yes, I do." She looked up at him, took a breath, and continued, "I trust you, Brandon. The only reason I'm afraid to tell you is that I'll be risking your life even more."

"We're in this together, Anna. You have to realize that. Whatever it was your father did, he will assume you've already told me."

She nodded and swallowed. "Sarah said my father sent her away when she heard my mother in labor. She was to stay upstairs with my brother and me. She heard a car, assumed it was Dr. Ivers coming to deliver the baby since my father hadn't taken my mother to the clinic in Antelope Flats or the hospital in Sheridan."

She fingered the worn edge of the envelope for a moment. "Sarah heard the baby cry and was relieved. She'd been worried about my mother. She hadn't been well. But that wasn't the only reason she'd been worried. She'd heard my father and mother arguing, my mother saying that the baby wasn't his and as soon as it was born, she was going to leave him."

Brandon braced himself, afraid of where she was going with this.

"My brother and I were both asleep, so she sneaked down the stairs, wanting to see my new baby sister or brother. But as she reached the bottom of the stairs, she heard my mother crying, pleading with my father 'not to do it.' Sarah hid as my father let Dr. Niles French come in. She heard my father tell him that the baby was stillborn and that it was time to take my mother."

Anna stopped and took another breath. It came out like a sob. "Sarah knew the baby hadn't been stillborn. She'd heard it cry. She hurried up the stairs. She didn't hear all of the conversation, just pieces of it because my mother was hysterical, pleading and begging with my father not to send her to Brookside."

"Brookside?" Brandon echoed. "The old mental institution?"

ABE CARMICHAEL had retired a good twenty years ago, but he was easy to track down since he hadn't gone far from Antelope Flats. Cash found the former sheriff sitting on his porch overlooking the river.

"Murder at Brookside? Oh, I remember it well," Abe said. "Hell of a thing."

Cash didn't know why he was bothering asking. What could a twenty-year-old murder have to do with Emma Ingles's murder?

Nothing.

And yet he couldn't let Emma's death go. The only connection was Brookside. But he'd learned to follow any lead that presented itself. His gut told him to follow this one.

"Do you remember much about it?" Cash asked.

Abe chuckled. He was a big man with a head of snow-white hair and bushy eyebrows. "Son, you never forget the cases you couldn't solve. They haunt you the rest of your life. This one was especially tragic. Big news at the time. The woman was murdered in her bed late at night. Room 9B. What made it so sensational was the fact that she was in the criminally insane wing."

"I don't understand."

"That section was locked up tighter than a drum. Only a few people even had keys to that wing. Plus the patients' rooms were also locked—and padded. No windows."

"So it had to be someone who had a key, someone who worked there," Cash said, finally understanding. "That had to narrow down the suspects."

"One of the attendants committed suicide not long after that," Abe said. "He left a note saying he was sorry. Nothing more."

Cash heard it in his voice. "But you don't believe he killed her."

"Never bought it. I think the real killer got away with it, but under the circumstances, without a motive, there was nothing I could do. You see, the woman was a Jane Doe. One of the doctors from Brookside found her wandering down the highway, crazier than crazy, and violent, too. The doctor just put her in that wing for the night to protect her from herself and everyone until she could be identified."

"You never found out who she was?"

Abe sighed. "Never did. She was bludgeoned to death that night. No way to make any kind of ID on her face or dental records."

Cash winced.

"It was a horrible thing. Still gives me nightmares. She's buried at the cemetery as Jane

Doe. I go up there every once in a while," Abe said. "Someone's been putting flowers on her grave for years."

Chapter Nine

Anna moved to the window overlooking the lake. Brandon stared at her slim back, too shocked to speak.

"Sarah says she never saw my mother again," Anna continued. "She sneaked back upstairs and pretended she knew nothing. The next morning, my father said the baby was stillborn and that my mother had left. No one was to ever mention her name in the house again or speak of the baby."

Brandon had heard about Anna's mother, Helena VanHorn. The woman was said to have been beautiful, with long black hair and a face like an angel. Obviously that's where Anna had gotten her beauty. But like everyone else, he'd heard that she'd run off. He hadn't known anything about a baby.

"Sarah never breathed a word, afraid of what my father would do to her. She left his employ shortly after that. She was dying when she wrote the letter and said she couldn't go to her grave with the secret. She'd heard I wrote for a newspaper in Maine and sent it there. But the letter got lost and didn't find me until nine years later."

Her story left him horrified. "The nanny's sure she heard the baby cry?"

"Yes. She was in a room directly above my mother's," Anna said.

"What happened to the baby's body?" he asked joining her at the window.

She shook her head. "I can only assume he got rid of it and locked my mother up in Brookside."

"Is it possible she's still alive?" Brandon asked.

"I doubt it. When Brookside closed, my father would have made sure she was never allowed to tell her story and there was no other place for her to go that he wouldn't be found out."

Brandon went cold inside at even the thought that any of this could be true. Mason VanHorn had a reputation for being a bastard and Brandon had seen firsthand how vindictive he could be. But he couldn't imagine the man doing something so heinous to his own wife.

"You don't believe it, do you?" she said, putting the envelope away. He could hear the hurt in her tone.

"I'm sorry, but you have to admit this is one

hell of an accusation. You're sure that this woman who wrote the letter didn't get it all wrong? For all you know, she might have been suffering from dementia. None of this might be true."

"That was my first thought. That's why I contacted Sarah's niece, who was with her when she died. Sarah was rational and very much in control of her senses when she wrote the letter. The niece didn't know what was in the letter, but had mailed it at her aunt's request nine years ago. If the letter hadn't gotten lost, I might have been able to talk to Sarah before she died."

Brandon moved around the room, too restless to sit. "My God, do you realize what you're accusing your father of here?"

"Yes. And not just my father. He had to have had help that night."

"Dr. Ivers would never go along with this," Brandon said.

Anna nodded. "I called Dr. Ivers. He said he didn't even know my mother was pregnant. So it must have been Dr. French who ordered the bed rest and delivered the baby. It was right after he left that Sarah said she didn't hear the baby cry again. She never saw the body. She just assumed my father had taken it out somewhere and buried it."

If she was right, Mason VanHorn had gotten away with murder—and much worse. "What about this Dr. French?"

"I gave his name to the private investigator I hired and now she's missing." She looked at him as if to say, how can you not believe me? "Before that, she was able to verify that Dr. French *was* on staff at the Brookside Mental Institution during that time."

"Twenty-seven years ago." Brandon raked a hand through his hair. "Was Lenore able to verify that your mother was a patient?"

"No, unfortunately the hospital was privately owned and when it suddenly closed, the records were lost. At least, that's what we've been led to believe."

"You think someone has them?" he asked in surprise.

"My father would have made sure my mother's medical file never got into the wrong hands. But also to make sure Dr. French never got a guilty conscience and decided to talk."

"That's what you were looking for in the safe."

She nodded. "I know my father has the records. They would implicate Dr. French."

"It would also implicate him."

"Yes. Kind of a Mexican standoff."

"How do you hope to prove any of this without records and the only witness dead?"

"The only witness isn't dead. Dr. French was in the room when the baby was born. I assume my father was also." She shivered. "I used to have nightmares that one day Dr. French would come for me, too."

He took her in his arms. He wanted to tell her that Dr. French would never get his hands on her. But if she was right, if her father had gotten rid of not only a baby but her mother with the help of Dr. French, and now both men knew she was on to them, then her life was in danger.

"Let's go see if we can find that private investigator," Brandon said, wanting to keep moving.

ANNA WATCHED the beach as they crossed the lake to the marina, half-afraid she would see her father or one of his flunkies waiting for them on the other side. Or worse, Dr. French.

But no one paid any attention to them as they tied up the boat, got into her rented black pickup and headed for Sheridan, Wyoming, and the motel where Lenore Johnson had been registered.

"I still think we should go to my brother with this," Brandon said.

"Cash is already looking for Lenore Johnson, the private investigator I hired," she said.

He had the pickup window down, the summer air blowing in. The cloudless day reminded him of cherry Popsicles.

"According to the agency, he will file a missing person's report in forty-eight hours," she said. "I have that long to get some proof."

Brandon couldn't see how after all these years she would ever find the proof.

"They will be running scared now," she said as she drove south down the two-lane. "That's why I called Dr. French and left a message telling him I was coming for him. But they will think they can handle me. They know I don't have any evidence."

"You contacted Dr. French?" he asked in surprise, glancing over at her. "Wait a minute, you're using yourself as bait. You *expect* them to come after you."

She smiled through her tears. "I have to do this. I owe it to my mother and the sibling I lost."

He understood. But how much did a child owe a parent? He thought of his own mother. "She wouldn't want to see you get killed, though."

"I just want to rattle them. It might be the

only justice I get. They won't kill me. Not unless they think I really do have something against them."

"Yeah," he said. "That's what worries me." If VanHorn had gotten rid of a baby he believed wasn't his, and had his wife locked up in Brookside for years and possibly had her murdered when the place closed, why wouldn't he kill again to hide his crimes?

"Did you ask your father about this?"

Anna nodded. "He told me the same story he'd told Sarah."

"I always thought he idolized you," Brandon said.

"When I was little. But something changed. The day I turned ten, he told me I was going away to school. I cried and pleaded with him to let me stay. Maybe the mistake I made was telling him that one day I would marry a cowboy and live on the ranch." Tears welled again in her eyes. "I think I saw it in his face that day. He never let me come back after that. Not even for a visit."

He heard the bitterness in her voice—and the longing. "You were just a kid. Would you have really come back to the ranch if he'd let you?"

"In a heartbeat. I love the ranch. It was the only place I ever wanted to be and he knew that," she said. "I used to think he didn't want me around because I looked too much like my mother, that it hurt him too much to see me."

"And now?"

"Now I think he kept me away so I'd never find out the truth."

Brandon hated the pain he heard in her voice. Damn Mason VanHorn for hurting his daughter—not to mention the other crimes he might have committed.

"If we can find the private investigator you hired…"

She nodded and smiled through her tears. "From that day on the curb when I shared my Popsicle with you, I knew I could count on you."

His gaze locked with hers and he felt desire course through his veins. He wished her eyes weren't that honey color or her hair so dark and luxurious or her body so lush. He wished her lips weren't bow-shaped or her laugh so musical. He wished he didn't want her so badly.

Because no matter how this ended, he could never have her. Not the way he wanted her. Forever.

AT THE SHADY REST Motor Inn, Anna told him that the motel clerk said she never checked out but all of her belongings were out of the room the next morning. "I was staying at the same motel in case she came back. She never did."

"What about her rental car?" he asked. "I assume she flew into Billings and rented a car there. That's what most people do since there isn't a commercial airport near here."

"I checked with her office. She always rents from the same agency. The car hasn't been returned."

"Okay, what about flights?" he asked.

"She hasn't used her return ticket, her office said."

"Well, maybe we can take a look at the room she stayed in. I know it's a long shot." He opened the pickup door. She was already out by the time he came around to her side, and headed for the motel office.

Anna knew he was hoping that Lenore would turn up safe and sound and provide an explanation for everything—one that didn't involve her father. She felt her own hopes of that slipping away. Lenore Johnson was either in trouble—or way past it. Anna blamed herself for involving the private investigator.

Inside the office, the clerk at the desk let them have the key to the room Lenore Johnson had rented but warned it had been cleaned.

"Were you working when Ms. Johnson was a guest here?" Brandon asked.

The young woman shook her head. "Jo was. She'll be in soon if you want to talk to her."

They took the key and walked down the cracked sidewalk to Room 12. The door creaked as Brandon opened it. Anna stepped inside the room, which was identical to the one she'd rented.

She looked under the bed while Brandon searched the bathroom and small closet. Nothing.

When they returned the key to the office, Jo had taken over the desk.

"Sure, I remember her," the older woman behind the counter told them. "Haven't seen her since Saturday, though, when she came into the office for directions."

"Directions?" Anna and Brandon both echoed.

The woman behind the counter laughed. "You two been married long? Pretty soon you'll be finishing each other's sentences."

"We're not married," Anna said, feeling shy. She didn't dare look at Brandon.

"Oh, sorry. You just seemed like such a perfect couple," the woman said almost dreamily.

"Lenore Johnson asked for directions, you said," Brandon reminded her.

"Oh, yeah. Come to think of it, I thought it was strange." The woman shrugged. "But hey, that's what I'm here for, renting rooms and giving directions." She sighed and looked at them, and must have realized they were still waiting. "She wanted to know how to get to the old Brookside Mental Institution."

SHERIFF CASH MCCALL spent the day working on the Emma Ingles case, as well as trying to track down the Virginia private investigator, Lenore Johnson.

He'd come up empty and was about to give up when he got a call from a friend of Emma Ingles.

Her name was Betty Osborne, she was seventy-six and made the best sweet pickles in the county. She had dozens of blue ribbons from the fair to prove it.

"I was just thinking about Emma today," Betty said, "and I knew I had to call you. I remembered something she'd said to me after she took that horrible job up there at Brookside."

He waited.

"She only took it because she needed the money. It's a crime what social security pays."

"Something she said to you?" he prodded gently.

"Yes. I don't think she minded the work. All she had to do was be there. She watched a lot of television, you know. I can't imagine being up there alone at night. Gives me chills just to think about it. You know, Emma almost married my second cousin, so we've been friends for years."

Cash was beginning to think he'd have to remind Betty again when she said, "Emma told me she heard voices coming from that wing where that woman was killed. You know, the one who was horribly murdered all those years ago."

"Voices?" He'd heard stories of the place being haunted for years. This was nothing new.

"Hushed voices," Betty said. "Like someone inside one of those padded cells in that disturbed wing. Someone crying out for help."

"I HAVE TO GET INSIDE Brookside," Anna told Brandon as they left the motel office. She could tell that the last thing Brandon wanted to do was go to Brookside. She was dreading it more than she wanted to admit. But if Lenore had been headed there right before she went missing, then maybe the answer to her disappearance was also there.

"Why do I get the feeling that you have a plan?" he asked grinning over at her. "A plan I'm going to hate."

She smiled. "Sorry, but I need you to pretend you want to buy the place."

"It's for *sale?*"

"A local Realtor is handling it for the state. Haven't been many takers, I guess," she said.

"I would assume not. It's just a huge white elephant out in the middle of nowhere," Brandon said.

She figured that, like her, he'd heard the stories about the place. When she'd asked about Brookside, every waitress and motel clerk had a horror story to tell.

Brandon opened the passenger-side door of the pickup for her, but something caught her eye. A headline in a newspaper box near where he'd parked the pickup.

Like a sleepwalker, she moved toward the newspaper box: Brookside Security Woman's Death Ruled A Homicide.

Anna felt Brandon come up beside her. "Do you see that? Do you think it could have anything to do with Lenore's disappearance? It says Emma Ingles worked at Brookside and was killed sometime during the night. That was the same day Lenore went missing."

Brandon sighed. "All roads seem to lead to Brookside."

"According to locals, the place is haunted," she said, and climbed into the pickup.

He slid behind the wheel. "You don't believe in ghosts." He made it sound as if he were waiting for her to reassure him of that.

"If there is something going on at Brookside, it isn't ghosts who are doing it," she said as she handed him her cell phone.

"Cell phones don't work out here."

"Only in some places. Also depends on the phone." She rattled off the Realtor's number. "He'll believe you want to buy the place quicker than he will me."

She watched him tap in the numbers. "Don't mention me. I want to do some exploring on my own while you keep him busy."

"Great idea," he said sarcastically, then, "Hello, Frank Yarrow? I'm interested in Brookside. I understand it's for sale. Yes, my name is Brandon McCall. Actually, my family is interested in purchasing it."

Anna nodded her approval.

Yarrow agreed to change his schedule and meet Brandon at Brookside in forty minutes.

"That will give us time to look around outside the place," Anna said.

Brandon shifted into gear, heading for the isolated old mental hospital as the sun dipped behind the mountains and the day grew cool and dark.

Chapter Ten

Brandon drove out of Sheridan, following the Tongue River as it wound its way north. The road rose into foothills; huge cottonwoods grew at the river's edge, tall gray sage dotted the arid landscape as the land ran from the river toward the Bighorn Mountains.

"I don't like the idea of you alone in that place," he said.

She smiled and touched his cheek with her fingers. "I won't be alone. You and the Realtor will be in there with me. If I need you, I'll holler."

He didn't look convinced, but she knew he would do it. He would do anything for her, she thought.

Even risk his life.

"Thank you," she said beside him.

He shot her a look, his gaze softening. He grinned at her and reached for her hand, giving it a squeeze. "I haven't pulled it off yet. Thank me when you find some evidence that will put an end to this."

"Can you fix the door so we can get back in later tonight if we have to?"

He nodded. That place was spooky as hell in the daylight. He didn't even want to think about going up there at night.

Realtor Frank Yarrow had been beside himself at the thought of selling Brookside. And Brandon doubted it was just for the commission. Yarrow had hesitated a little about showing the place, mentioning that it would be getting dark soon.

Brandon had to smile. Obviously the Realtor didn't like going up there at night, either, but who could blame him?

Fifteen miles out of town, Brandon turned onto the dirt road. There had once been a weathered sign that said nothing more than Brookside, but it had been gone for years.

He looked over and saw Anna gripping the handle on the dash as he started up the winding dirt road. Rockslides and weeds had narrowed the road to only a single lane in places.

The sun had set. In the twilight, the mountains were purple. Below them, the Tongue River twisted through deep green grass and huge leafy cottonwoods. A flock of geese made a dark V of flapping wings against the horizon.

The highway disappeared behind them as the narrow road rounded the mountain, culminating in a half-dozen switchback curves all headed upward. On one side of the road, there was mountain; on the other, rocky cliffs that dropped down thousands of feet. There were no guardrails. No trees. Nothing to stop you if you drove off the road but the rocky bottom below.

As he came around the last turn, Brookside rose up, black against the dying sunset, a huge looming brick edifice three stories high.

Brandon heard Anna gasp and realized this was the first time she'd ever seen it. Brookside had that effect. Even when you knew the place was just over the rise, it always came as a surprise. Partly because of the isolation. Partly because of the ominous-looking shape of it.

The building was an odd U shape, with the two wings jutting back from each side. The high metal fence had three razor wire strands on top that only a fool didn't know once kept things in, not out.

The iron gate had long since been torn down. Brandon drove through but didn't go up the circular drive, now filled with weeds. He parked a good distance away in a flat spot that was once a lawn.

The windows along one wing had the sun reflecting off them, making them look like golden eyes. The rest of the building was dark. No other cars were parked out front.

He turned to Anna. "Are you sure you want to do this?"

Anna sat for a long moment just staring at the building, trying hard not to imagine her mother locked inside it. She opened her door in answer to Brandon's question and stepped out before she lost her nerve.

Cool shadows pooled around the huge place. Dozens of patients had once lived inside. How many of them were like her mother? she hated to think. This far from everything, few families would ever come to visit. Had that been the idea?

She heard Brandon get out of the pickup as she closed her door and started toward the side. She wanted to take a look out back. The doors would be locked, so she would have to wait until the Realtor arrived to sneak inside. Not that she expected to find anything on the exterior. She'd be lucky to find anything inside.

But she had to confront this horrible place and the fears that had lived inside her since she'd learned about the night Dr. French came to her house and took her mother away.

As she reached the cracked concrete walkway, she heard Brandon come up behind her.

"Watch your step," he warned. "There could be rattlesnakes up here."

Rattlesnakes were the least of her fears.

The broken concrete path led around to the back. She stopped at the edge of the worn brick wall and stared at what had once been an orchard. There were dozens of dead apple trees, their limbs stark and dark against the last of the day's light.

She glanced at the back of the building, a glare keeping her from seeing into the dusty barred windows of the north wing. Had her mother's room looked out on the orchard? Or had she been in the windowless rooms on the south wing?

Brandon walked to the back door. "Look, there's a buzzer." He pushed it and she heard the faint sound echo through the empty building. She was glad he didn't press it again. The sound set her teeth on edge.

"I think I've seen enough," she said.

He nodded and took her arm as they maneuvered along the side.

She would not cry. She would *not* cry. Her

eyes burned. She breathed in the mountain air, filling her lungs with it. In the distance, she heard the sound of a vehicle coming up the road, and went to hide.

BRANDON STOOD OUTSIDE Brookside as a fancy new rig rolled up and an older man in a brown suit climbed out. Few people in this part of the country wore actual suits. Western sports jackets with jeans and boots, yes. Suits, no.

Frank Yarrow wore a suit that didn't quite fit his squat body. He tugged at his collar, his thick finger digging into the flushed flesh of his neck. His toupee was dyed jet-black and sat like a squirrel on his slick bald head, the corners lifting in the breeze.

"Frank Yarrow," he said by way of introduction, extending his hand. "And you must be Brandon McCall. Heard a lot about the McCalls. Sundown Ranch, right? Your brother's the sheriff up that way."

"Right." He could see Yarrow already mentally spending his commission.

"Well, let's have a look inside," Yarrow said with less enthusiasm. He pulled a ring of keys from his pocket. "Great space, and quite the view from here." If you didn't notice the fence.

Brandon followed him, looking around for Anna. He didn't see her, but he knew she hadn't gone far. It made him nervous leaving her to her own devices, but the only other option was breaking in, and he quickly realized that would be impossible. The place was like a fortress.

He wished he could have gone to his brother about this. But there was no chance Cash could get a court order without evidence.

After digging out a huge key ring, Yarrow opened the front door. Brandon motioned him to go in first. He'd picked up a small chunk of wood out back. He took it out of his pocket now, dropping it as the door closed behind him but didn't latch.

"This is a great price for this much space," Yarrow said, waiting for him in the entry, his voice echoing in the emptiness. The Realtor seemed nervous. Not half as nervous as Brandon was.

"I'd like to start at the top and work my way down if that's all right," Brandon said, following Anna's instructions.

"All right. The elevator—"

"Would you mind if we took the stairs?" Brandon asked. "I have this thing about elevators." They were too fast and he needed to buy Anna as much time as possible.

"All right." More enthusiasm waning. "It is three stories at the center, you realize."

Brandon nodded. "We're in no hurry, right?"

"Of course not. It's just a little hard to see once it gets dark. Not a lot of lighting," he said glancing up the dimly lit stairs as if he was worried what might be waiting up there for them.

ANNA WASN'T ANXIOUS to see the inside of Brookside. The name made it sound like a spa rather than a mental hospital.

She steeled herself for what she might find as she waited until she was sure Brandon would have had time to get the Realtor started up the stairs before she approached the front door. True to his word, Brandon had managed to prop the door open for her.

She stepped inside, assaulted first by the stagnant smell of a long-ago locked-up building, and other smells—she didn't want to know what they were.

The moment the door closed behind her, she heard faint echoes, felt the oppression. It threatened to immobilize her. She tried not to breathe, not to think.

How many years had her mother been in here? Anna couldn't bear to think what atrocities her mother had been subjected to once she was locked inside this building. Was she just warehoused, a prisoner with a life sentence? Or had her father let them do horrible treatments on her? Just how high was the Van-Horn price for being unfaithful, she wondered, raw with pain and anger.

She tried to remember the details of the map she'd gotten from the county as she glanced down the hallway to the south wing. The double doors were chained and locked. She didn't want to know.

The other wing was open.

She hurried down the hallway toward the open wing, past the small enclosed office, the mesh window winking under the dim lights as she passed.

If she remembered correctly, the door to the basement was down the hallway on a corridor in the wing of that side of the building.

She could hear clanking, echoing noises, and would have sworn that not all of them were coming from upstairs where Brandon and the Realtor would be now.

Almost at the end of the hall, she stopped. Nothing but barred or windowless room after room. Could she be wrong? Could the way to the basement be in the other wing? The locked wing?

Her heart fell at the thought. All of this would have been for nothing.

She glanced at her watch. She didn't have much time. The door had to be here. She rushed down the hall, trying not to make any more noise than was possible.

The hallway was long, the linoleum worn and discolored. Doors yawned, open to the patient rooms. She didn't look inside, didn't want to imagine what her mother's life must have been like here.

Almost to the end, she spotted a door that was larger than the others. She could hear voices so faint they sounded like whispers. Let it be Brandon and the Realtor. Not the voices of those poor souls who had walked these worn halls.

The wider door opened into a cavernous dark hole. She flicked on the flashlight and shone it into the darkness. Stairs.

A fetid smell gagged her. She took shallow breaths. The air coming up the stairs was colder, damper, the horrid smell stronger. Not just moldy. Not just stagnant, but something stronger. Something dead.

BRANDON LED THE WAY up the stairs to the third floor, going as slowly as possible, pretending to study the stairwell as he climbed. Frank followed, quickly winded. Clearly, the man got little exercise other than climbing in and out of his car to show real estate.

At the third-floor landing, Brandon stopped to wait for him. Where was Anna? By now, she would be in the building. He hated this more than he wanted to admit. This place gave him the creeps. He could just imagine what it must be doing to her.

Worse, he worried about what she might find. Or what might find her.

"All the floors are almost identical," Yarrow said when he'd caught his breath. He sounded bitter that they'd had to climb the stairs rather than take the elevator.

Brandon smiled and pushed open the door to the third floor. "I guess we're about to see if that is true."

Unfortunately, Yarrow was right. The floor was just a long hallway with bare, uninteresting, windowless or barred rooms off each side. The smell—let alone the thought of who had occupied these rooms and for how long—was enough to make Brandon want to rush through this inspection of the building. He had to keep reminding himself that he was buying time for Anna.

He prayed her information about her mother was wrong. He feared what it would do to her if she found proof that her mother had been housed here out of vengeance.

"As you can see, there are lots of possibilities with something this size," Yarrow said. "It could make a great out-of-the-way hotel. Even a resort."

Right. Yarrow was kidding himself if he thought he could ever dump this place.

"I understand the state owns the building and land now," Brandon said.

"They're very receptive to an offer. They were forced to take it over when it closed. However, there are some restrictions on what can be done with the building," Yarrow said.

"What kind of restrictions?" Not that he really cared. But if he was seriously interested in purchasing the place, it was a question he would ask.

"The building has to be saved if at all possible. It is structurally sound and a historical site."

Brandon stopped walking and looked at the man in surprise. "Why would anyone buy the building and tear it down?"

"One potential buyer was turned down because his plans included razing the site," Yarrow said.

"Really? Anyone I know?"

Yarrow wagged his head. "I'm not allowed to say." He started walking toward the elevator. "The next floor is identical but I'm sure you'll want to see it, as well."

A chill curled around Brandon's neck, as if a cold draft had crept down the hall after him, and yet there were no windows that actually opened.

He hurried after Yarrow, anxious to get out of this place as quickly as possible.

Hurry, Anna.

"You don't mind if we take the stairs, do you?" he said, and held open the stairway door for the Realtor.

ANNA TRIED the light switch at the top of the stairs. Nothing. She shone her flashlight down the concrete steps to the bottom. Slowly, she descended the stairs, forced to keep the light on the steps ahead of her rather than the darkness beyond it.

At the bottom, she stopped and shone the flashlight beam around the room. Other than for support beams, the huge space appeared to be almost empty except for some old bed frames, a few mattresses and some metal chairs against one wall.

The smell was much stronger down here. She covered her mouth with her free hand, her eyes stinging.

At a sound, she swung the flashlight beam in that direction. Pipes. She held her breath, listening. *Drip*. A water leak. *Drip*. Nothing more. But she kept the light on the pipes for a moment as she tried to calm herself.

She shone the light around the perimeter of the room again, hoping she might find a filing cabinet. Or boxes. Or something that might hold old files. She knew there was little chance the files would be down here. The place had been closed for years. Any evidence had long since been lost. Or taken.

As her flashlight beam skimmed along the outer walls, she saw that several of the basement windows had been broken. No bars. Access if she had to come back. The light skittered along the wall. She stopped. Behind one of the bed frames she saw the top of what could be the outline of a door frame.

Cautiously, she stepped off the last stair onto the concrete. If the files had been stored down here, who knew what kind of shape they might be in, even if she did find them.

But she had to hold out hope. If she was right, her mother had spent the last years of her life in this building.

She had to put the flashlight down on the concrete floor, the beam aimed at the bed frame as she tried to pull it away from the doorway. The bed frame was heavy—dense metal and awkward to move.

It finally budged. She scraped the bed frame across the floor far enough that she could see she'd been right. A door.

Picking up the flashlight, she shone the light on the door. Her fingers closed over the knob. She held her breath, saying a silent prayer as she tried it. The knob turned in her hand, the door swung open with a groan and Anna blinked in shock as she found herself looking into another smaller room—this one filled with rows of old gray metal filing cabinets.

BRANDON STARED DOWN the second-floor hallway. It was indeed identical to the floor above. He couldn't stall much longer. Yarrow kept looking toward the barred windows. Twilight had turned the mountains deep purple. Huge pools of darkness hung in the pines. It would be full-dark before they got out of here at this rate.

"The first floor is all we have left to see," Yarrow said. "That's where the office is and the north wing, which was once used as a dormitory for nurses and students."

As far as Brandon could tell, the place had been completely cleaned out. He doubted there was anything to find. He heard sounds on other floors and wondered if Yarrow heard them, too. Maybe Anna wasn't making the noises. Now there was a frightening thought.

Yarrow held open the first-floor stairway door. Brandon couldn't put it off any longer. He headed down the stairs. At the bottom, he looked around for Anna and fortunately didn't see her.

"What's down that wing?" he asked, seeing the chained and locked double doors.

"Patient rooms. Why don't we go on down to the basement first while there is still a little light?" Yarrow said. "I brought a flashlight."

"Do you mind if I see this wing first?" Brandon asked. "I'm trying to get a feel for the size of this place."

Yarrow obviously did mind, but he tried not to show it. "There is nothing down there but rooms. The basement contains the boiler, a storage room. Plenty of room for a laundry."

"You have a key to this wing?" Brandon said, stepping over to pick up the chain and inspect the padlock.

Still Yarrow hesitated. "That wing was where the criminally insane were kept. The rooms are padded. Soundproof."

"Interesting," Brandon said, thinking it was

the last place on earth he really wanted to go. "Why is it still locked up like this?"

"Kids. They're like ghouls. Same with some of the security people. Just best to keep the curious out of here," Yarrow said. "A bit morbid, if you ask me."

"You have a key?" Brandon asked again. "I might as well see it all." Was this the wing where Dr. French had brought Anna's mother?

With obvious hesitancy, Frank pulled out the keys and dug through until he found one that fit the lock attached to the chain.

The padlock opened, the chain fell away and he pushed open the double doors, motioning Brandon to go first.

Brandon looked down the dim hallway of padded rooms. A thought struck him. What if, when he stepped through those doors, Yarrow locked them behind him? It was so ridiculous he almost laughed. Almost.

RUSHING TO the filing cabinets, Anna jerked open the first drawer. The moment she felt it slide toward her, she knew. It was empty. She tried another and another. All empty. Her heart sank. Nothing.

She stumbled back a few feet, letting the light flicker over the old metal file cabinets, fighting the urge to cry. The evidence *had* been here. How long ago had the files been cleaned out? If the state hadn't taken possession of them, then who had? Maybe they had just been destroyed. Maybe there was no possible hope of ever proving her mother had been here.

But she knew in her heart that her father had the file she was looking for. Still, she'd hoped there might be something....

She opened each file cabinet drawer. Empty. Empty. Empty. Her fingers felt grimy. She wiped them on her jeans as she moved to the last of the file cabinets.

Time was running out. She couldn't keep looking. Brandon would be making his way in this direction with the Realtor.

Why was she wasting her time? All the file cabinets were empty. There was nothing here. She started to open the top drawer, already hearing the empty clank as she touched the handle. She froze. Then slowly, she shined the light on what had caught her eye.

Something had fallen between the last two metal filing cabinets. Not a file. She could see that. But what looked like a thin bound ledger.

Laying the flashlight on top of one of the other file cabinets, the beam angled away from her eyes, she shoved the last file cabinet aside, then moved the next one until there was space enough to reach in.

Retrieving the flashlight, she shone it into the space before she bent to retrieve the dusty ledger and, with trembling fingers, opened it. At first, she didn't have any idea what it was. The only numbers seemed to be times and dates. On the left were names, then times, then signatures.

Her heart leaped to her throat. It was a log book. Visitors had been required to log in.

Hurriedly, she checked the dates. This book could have been used during the time she believed her mother was incarcerated here.

But if no one knew her mother was alive, then she wouldn't have had any visitors. Her heart fell at the realization.

She started to close the book when something caught her eye. Room 9B. Only the initials: HV. Helena VanHorn? Her gaze shot over to the signature of the person who'd visited the patient.

All breath rushed from her. She grabbed the edge of the file cabinet. Spots appeared before her eyes and she thought she might pass out.

She'd seen this almost illegible signature on the checks she'd received for spending money from the time she was ten until she completed college and began returning the checks—uncashed—in an envelope with nothing else. The same way the checks had arrived.

The signature was Mason VanHorn's.

Chapter Eleven

Anna stared at the signature. He'd come to visit her mother? She quickly thumbed through the book and found more entries. Why would he visit her? Just to taunt her?

A noise overhead startled her. She had to get out of here. She turned and, clutching the ledger to her, made her way to the door to the huge room.

The smell was much stronger in this room. She glanced toward the mattress against the wall and thought she heard the scurry of small feet. Mice. She cringed at the thought of what might be living there—worse, what had died there. That corner was definitely where the smell was coming from.

She shone the light in that direction. There was something back in the corner under one of the mattresses. She stepped closer, suddenly afraid. There was more room behind the mattress than she'd first thought. Enough room for a body. A body would decay quickly down here.

Her mind recoiled at the thought. The smell was overpowering now. She moved a little closer, bracing herself as she reached out to draw back the mattress.

THE WING for the criminally insane was worse than anything Brandon had seen. The rooms were padded, dark, small, windowless. They instantly gave him claustrophobia and made him sick to his stomach at just the thought of being locked in there.

He tried not to show the panic he was feeling just being in this wing. Sweat broke out on his forehead despite how cool it was. He wiped at it. "It's hot in here," he said, seeing that Yarrow had noticed.

"Have you seen enough?" the Realtor asked.

"What's in there?" Brandon asked at the closed door of Room 9B.

"Just another room," the Realtor said, trying the door. It was locked. The small window in the door had been covered over, making it impossible to see inside.

Anna was somewhere in the building looking for the lost files. Was it possible they were in this room? Why else lock up the wing with a chain and padlock and this room? And cover the window? "You have a key for this room?"

"I'm sure it's just another room like the others," Yarrow said, sounding more than ready to get out of here.

Brandon couldn't have agreed more. But he wanted to see what was in this room. He had to, for Anna's sake. Then he just wanted out of here.

He needed fresh air so badly it was all he could do not to take off at a run for the front door.

Yarrow smiled to cover his irritation and began to go through his keys. He tried one after another. "That's funny. I don't seem to have a key to this room. But I'm sure there is nothing in there."

As Anna pulled back the corner of the mattress, she saw what at first appeared to be a pile of rags. Her heart jumped to her throat, choking off her startled cry as she saw the head.

It was dark, the hair matted, the eyes lifeless. She let go of the corner of the mattress and stumbled back, covering her mouth and nose with her hand.

A coyote. It must have been sick or hurt, came through one of the broken windows at the back and curled up and died here.

A door slammed overhead, making her jump. She could hear footfalls above her. She'd been down here too long. If she didn't get out now, she would be caught leaving the building.

She turned and ran to the stairs, slowing to hide the sound of her footsteps as she ascended the steps to the first floor.

As she carefully pushed open the door, she heard Brandon's voice. Her spirits buoyed at just the sound. He and the Realtor were at the other end of the building.

She practically ran down the hallway toward the front door. She tried not to look in any of the rooms, tried not to let herself imagine what it would have been like for her mother spending the rest of her life locked up here.

As she turned the corner in the hallway, she saw Brandon and the Realtor in the far wing, their backs to her.

She sprinted down the hall, past the vacant office to the front door. She slipped out and gasped for air, suddenly crying. The sobs rose from deep inside her, racking her body.

Her mother had definitely been in Brookside. She had no idea how many years she'd been imprisoned there. Or what had happened to her once inside. But her father couldn't lie to her any longer. She had the ledger. She knew!

She climbed into the pickup, curling onto the seat and closing the door softly behind her, unable to stanch the flood of tears. She cried for the mother she'd never really known, for the pain her mother must have suffered, for justice and finally for her father's soul.

Her cell phone rang.

She fished it out of her pocket in surprise. There was cell-phone service in Sheridan, but not around the lake or Antelope Flats. But apparently there was out here on this mountaintop.

She glanced at the number on the tiny screen, foolishly hoping it was Lenore Johnson, her private investigator.

It wasn't, of course.

It was her father, Mason VanHorn.

MASON VANHORN had gotten her cell-phone number from Anna's former boss. He held his breath, praying he could get her to meet him, praying he could convince her to stop this horrible vendetta against him. He had to convince her. The alternative was too horrible to even consider.

He was surprised when her cell phone rang instead of telling him she was out of the calling area or had her phone turned off.

He was even more surprised to hear her voice on the other end of the line.

"Christianna," he said on a surprised breath.

"I go by Anna now," she said, her voice cold and clipped.

"Anna." Why had she changed her name? Didn't she know how much that hurt him?

She *wanted* to hurt him. If she had her way, she would destroy him. The realization came with less shock than pain. His Chrissy. He'd done so many things wrong with her. Just as he had his son. He should never have had children. He realized that now. But he never dreamed he would have to raise them alone, never dreamed how his actions over the years would harm them.

He took a breath. Now that he had her on the line, he didn't know what to say. "Where are you?" He prayed she'd say Virginia.

"I'm at Brookside."

His heart lunged in his chest, knocking the breath from him.

"What? Nothing to say? I know you put my mother in here and I can prove it."

"We need to talk." He said, finally able to speak.

She laughed. The sound cut him like a blade. "So you can lie to me again?"

He closed his eyes, wiping his free hand over his face. "I lied to protect you."

"The way you protected my mother?"

"Chris—Anna, if you come out to the ranch, I will tell you the truth. I should have a long time ago, but I couldn't bring myself—"

"I'm going to expose your lies. You and Dr. French. If you think you can stop me the way you did the private investigator I hired, you're wrong. What did you do with her? Did you really think you could get away with it? Or are you planning to get rid of me, too?" Her voice broke.

He felt sick. "You have to know I would never hurt you."

"You have already hurt me. I'm going to destroy you the way you did my mother and the child she gave birth to. You killed them both. The baby quickly, my mother more slowly to punish her for her affair. Or are you going to try to deny that she had an affair and that the baby was another man's, the way you've denied everything else?"

He heard the pain and anger in her voice. It broke his heart. "No, I'm not going to deny it. Your mother did have an affair and became pregnant with another man's child."

He heard what could have been a sob on the

other end of the line. "But I didn't murder anyone." As he said the words he'd said to himself so many times over the last almost-thirty years, he heard the lie in his voice.

"Anna, please, if you don't want to come out to the ranch, then meet me somewhere. We have to talk."

"Meet you so you can dispose of me the way you did my mother? Or the private investigator I hired?"

He didn't think his heart could break any further, but he was wrong.

She was crying now, her words almost lost in her tears. "Turn yourself in. Don't make this any worse." The line went dead.

When he tried to call her back, she'd turned off her phone.

REALTOR FRANK YARROW nervously wiped his full upper lip. "Sorry, I guess I don't have a key for this room. The wind probably caught the door and when it shut, automatically locked it."

Right. A gust of wind in a wing where there were no windows?

"Wait a minute," he said. "Here it is." He slipped the key into the lock and turned it. The door to Room 9B swung open.

Brandon held his breath, half-afraid of what he would see.

"There, I told you. Just like all the other rooms," Yarrow said.

He stared at the small padded cell. Empty. Just like all the others. But the room had an odd smell. Almost like…perfume. He recoiled at the scent, not wanting to know about the woman who must have lived in 9B. How odd that the smell would still be here after all these years.

"When was the last time this room was occupied?" he asked Yarrow.

"Twenty years at least," the Realtor said. "Shall we check out the other wing?" He sounded anxious to get this over with.

"Did you notice the smell of perfume?" Brandon asked, unable to let it go.

Yarrow gave him a pitying look. "No."

Brandon followed him back through the double doors. He could see through the entry windows that it was dark outside. Behind him, he heard Yarrow start to padlock the chains together again.

"Is that necessary?" Brandon asked. "I mean, why keep that wing locked up?"

Yarrow looked down the long empty hallway. Clearly, he liked keeping it locked, probably for reasons he didn't even understand himself. He snapped the padlock into place. "The night security guards like it locked."

He just bet they did.

The other wing was nothing but empty rooms, a men's restroom and a ladies', each with a few stalls or urinals.

"This was the nurses' office," Frank said. The door to the office was open. It was the only room Brandon had seen that had furniture in it—and heat. There was a small television perched on a filing cabinet.

Brandon opened the filing cabinet. Empty. "Emma Ingles worked here?" he asked, trying the other drawers. All empty.

Yarrow cleared his throat. "Yes. Of course, her death had nothing to do with Brookside."

Of course.

"So there is a security guard every night," Brandon said, hoping he and Anna didn't have to come back, that she'd found what she was looking for. Or at least realized it wasn't in this drafty old horrible place.

Yarrow coughed. "Well, with Emma's unfortunate demise and Karl quitting without notice... Of course, I will get more security hired just as quickly as possible. Don't worry about that. No one can get in. The place is locked up tight. Have to be careful not to get locked in."

"I really don't need to see any more," Brandon said. Yarrow looked more than relieved.

They walked to the front door. It was dark outside, shadows moving in the breeze. Brandon held the door open. Yarrow rushed through almost at a trot. Brandon closed the door, the small piece of wood keeping it from locking just in case they had to come back. Or Anna was still inside.

"Well, thank you for showing it to me. I'd like to give it some thought. I'll get back to you." He shook Yarrow's hand.

"I think it could be a good investment for you and your family," Frank said as he started to get into his car. "Definite possibilities."

Brandon nodded, still unable to imagine what anyone would do with Brookside, given its history. But didn't all buildings come with a history, usually one the owner had no way of knowing?

Wisps of clouds brushed across the dark sky. A rim of gold shone over the mountains to the east where the moon would be rising. The air felt cold for this time of the year, but then they were at least a thousand feet higher up here than down by the lake.

Brandon pretended to study the hulking dark shape of the building as Yarrow drove off. The moment the Realtor was over the first hill, Brandon headed for the pickup. He opened the driver's-side door, the light coming on in the cab.

Anna was hunkered down on the seat in the darkness. She sat up and he saw her face.

Oh, God. "What happened?"

ANNA HALTINGLY TOLD HIM about the dead coyote she'd found and her father's phone call.

He pulled her into his arms, holding her tightly. "All I found was a locked room in the padded cell wing. At first Frank didn't have the key and I thought... But then he found it and the room was empty like all the others."

She pulled back. "What was the room number?"

"9B."

Anna thought her heart might stop. "That was my mother's room." She fumbled the ledger out from under the seat where she'd hidden it, opening it to the page where she'd found her mother's initials, pointing to the room number next to them. And her father's signature.

Brandon stared down at the ledger in obvious shock. "You found this in the building?"

"Dropped between two file cabinets in the

basement. The files were all gone, but this proves that my mother was here."

"And that your father came to visit her." He sounded astonished, much as she had. He looked out through the windshield at Brookside. "Do you mind if we get out of here?"

She shook her head, closing the ledger as he turned off the dome light and started the truck.

As Brandon pulled away, she glanced back only once at the massive brick building and felt a chill quake through her. They'd left the door partially ajar. In case they had to come back.

MASON SAT IN THE DARK knowing what he had to do. Chrissy was with Brandon McCall. Who knew what lies McCall had told her? His daughter. He was going to lose her, too.

He closed his eyes and felt the burning tears behind his lids. He couldn't remember the last time he'd cried. Then he realized that, too, was a lie.

It was the night his beautiful wife gave birth to another man's baby.

He opened his eyes, wiped angrily at his tears as he picked up the phone and dialed Red Hudson's extension.

"Get up here!" he snapped, and hung up.

He had to stop Christianna before it was too

late. But first he would have to separate her from Brandon McCall. No matter what it took. The McCalls would love to see him destroyed. Especially Asa.

He heard Red come in the front door without knocking, heard the rapid thud of his footfalls and knew he'd made Red angry again. He wondered if he'd hired the wrong man for the job. He was about to find out.

Red's large frame filled his office doorway. "You drunk? Or just forgot how to turn on a light?"

Mason reached over and snapped on his desk lamp.

Red's expression changed from one of irritation to worry. "What's wrong?"

"You still haven't found McCall?"

Red shook his head. "Stick and Bubba found the camp where the two of them stayed last night. But they got away. I have men out looking for them."

Mason studied the man. The problem with Red was that he had scruples. But there'd been a time when he hadn't. And that was the leverage Mason had on the man. Unfortunately, Red was determined to change his life.

"Find out if they've gone to the McCall ranch. If not, then they have to be staying around here somewhere. Check motels and rentals. I need McCall out of the way."

Red raised a brow.

"All I want you to do is detain him. Put him in that old storage bin on the south end of the ranch. Make him comfortable. But make sure he doesn't leave until I give you the word."

Red said nothing.

"My daughter and I need to talk—without McCall. So I need you to find him. Turn over every rock in the county if that's what it takes."

"You're that sure she's still around?"

Mason nodded. He could see Red was wondering what she'd been doing in the house, in the safe. "I wasn't a very good father. She wants to hurt me."

Red shifted on his feet, obviously uncomfortable with Mason's confession.

"Maybe McCall tried to stop her and she hit him with that iron doorstop," Mason continued, knowing he had to get Red on his side. "Now he seems to be sympathizing with her. Or at the very least, trying to protect her from me."

Red shot up a brow. "Is that necessary?"

"She's my daughter. I love her more than my own life," Mason said without hesitation.

Red nodded. "I'll try to find them myself.

You do realize, though, that such an action might be considered kidnapping?"

Sarcasm. "Yes, I'm aware of that, but I don't think McCall will press charges. He was trespassing on my land just last night and helped a known vandal. Also, I think you might be right about him."

Red smiled but still looked skeptical.

"Just get McCall away from her. I'll take care of the rest."

Red stood for a moment, as if considering everything he'd been told, then slowly nodded. "I'll find them. But if anything happens to either of them, you're on your own."

Mason nodded. "Let me know as soon as you have him. Make sure my daughter is protected."

He watched Red leave. If anything happened to Brandon McCall, Red would go to the sheriff. Now Mason knew how much he could trust Red Hudson. Not very damned far.

But Mason wasn't worried about Red. No, his concern was with Niles French. The doctor was running scared and that made him dangerous. Very dangerous.

Dr. French would be looking for Christianna. Mason had to find her before he did.

Chapter Twelve

The lights from the pickup cut through the darkness as Brandon started down the narrow winding dirt road.

The night was black, the clouds low and dark. Behind the pickup, dust rose like ghosts chasing after them.

He tried not to drive too fast, but at the same time he wanted to put distance between them and Brookside.

Anna leaned back against the seat and closed her eyes. "I don't know what to think."

She'd found what appeared to be evidence that her mother had been in the institution. But even more disturbing was finding out that her father had visited Helena during that time.

"Are you all right?"

"Mmm," she said in answer.

He reached over to cover her hand with his free one. He gave her fingers a light squeeze.

A lone tear coursed down her cheek. He lifted his hand to thumb it away. He'd noticed earlier that she'd been crying, her face flushed, eyes red.

He hadn't said anything, not knowing really what to say. Just as he didn't know what to say now. The ledger seemed to confirm that her mother had been in Brookside—just as she'd feared. They still didn't know for how many years she was locked up there, or even if she still might be alive somewhere.

But the big question the ledger raised was why visit a woman Mason VanHorn supposedly hated so much he'd had locked up?

Brandon glanced back almost as if he thought some intangible evil might be chasing them. The set of headlights surprised him. Frank Yarrow had gone down first. And since there were no turnoffs and the road ended at Brookside, where had the vehicle come from?

There hadn't been another car at Brookside. At least not when they first got there. Was it possible someone had driven up while they were inside?

In the rearview mirror, he watched the lights growing brighter and brighter as the vehicle grew closer, coming up fast behind them.

Brandon touched his brakes, hoping the driver could see the flash of his brake lights through the dust. The car didn't slow. It was headed right for them.

"What is it?" Anna asked. She was sitting up, staring at him. She glanced back. "There's someone behind us?"

"Hang on!"

"He's going to ram us," Anna cried.

The cab filled with light as what appeared to be a black SUV smashed into the back of the pickup with a jarring crash.

There was no way to pull off the road or get away from the other vehicle. Brandon fought to keep the truck on the road as he went into another hairpin turn.

The SUV slammed into the pickup again, this time making it fishtail. The back tires slid toward the edge of the cliff. Brandon turned the wheel and righted the pickup, hitting the gas, hoping to put a little space between them.

Through the headlights, he could see another sharp curve coming up, remembered it from earlier, knew that was where the vehicle behind them would hit again.

On one side, he had the mountain; on the other, a cliff that dropped in a tumble of rocks.

He couldn't outrun the vehicle behind them and it would be suicide to try.

But the curve was coming up quickly and if he was hit from behind while in that tight curve— He had only one chance. He glanced over at Anna. "Brace yourself."

He punched the gas, spinning the rear wheels as he sped up, churning up as much dust as he could. The SUV's headlights disappeared behind them in the cloud of dust. He was almost to the curve. He couldn't see the SUV behind him but he knew it was there, probably coming up fast behind him again. The driver knew the road. He wasn't trying to scare them. He was trying to kill them.

Right before the curve, Brandon cut hard into the side of the mountain. Along with the initial impact came a shower of dirt and rocks that flew up over the top of the pickup.

"Hang on!" he yelled over the thunderous roar as the pickup dug into the mountainside, coming to rest precariously, leaning to one side. If it rolled, they were both dead. An instant later, they were struck from behind, only a glancing blow as the vehicle clipped the back bumper and scraped along the side of the truck as it careered past, taking the side mirror with it.

Anna let out a sound. Not a scream, but a cry as the other vehicle shot past, barely making the curve.

Brandon only got a glimpse of the dark-colored SUV, then it was gone.

"Are you all right?" he cried, looking over at Anna as dust and darkness settled over the pickup.

She nodded, her eyes wide in the lights from the dash. He reached over and cupped her pale face in his palm. "My God, you're hurt."

"It's nothing. I just hit my head on the window," she said. "Is he gone?"

Brandon nodded. "He's in front of us. He'll take off, afraid we'll come after him." He opened the glove box and pulled out a packet of tissues. "Here." He pressed several into her hand. "It's not bleeding badly, but I'm taking you to the clinic to have you checked out anyway."

He hurriedly shifted the pickup into reverse. The tires spun for a moment, then caught as he backed up onto the road and sat for a moment, trying to collect himself. That had been too close a call.

"He tried to kill us," she said, her voice growing stronger.

Brandon got the pickup moving, thankful he hadn't blown a tire or worse. He just wanted off this mountain and away from Brookside.

"MY FATHER DRIVES a dark-colored SUV," Anna said when they reached the highway. There was no sign of the vehicle that had tried to run them off the road.

Brandon looked over at her. "A lot of people drive dark-colored SUVs around here. Anyway, he had no way of knowing we were at Brookside."

She bit her lip, her eyes swimming in tears. She wiped at them. "When he called me, I told him where I was. He wanted to see me. He said if I'd meet him, he would tell me the truth."

Even in the dim light from the dashboard, she could see his shock.

"Don't jump to conclusions," he said. "Frank Yarrow could have told a number of people he was showing me the building. I don't believe the person driving that SUV was your father. He's in his sixties."

"And strong as an ox," she said.

"But he wouldn't try to kill you," Brandon said adamantly.

She wished she could be so sure.

At the clinic, he helped Anna inside against her protests that she was fine.

"Is Dr. Ivers here?" Brandon asked the receptionist. "Can you call him?"

"I'm here," said a voice behind them. Brandon turned to see Dr. *Taylor* Ivers. "What seems to be the problem?"

"She hit her head," Brandon said.

"It's nothing," Anna protested.

"Step in here, please," Dr. Taylor Ivers said as she drew back a curtain in the small emergency area. She let Anna pass, but stopped Brandon. "*You* may wait out there."

She closed the drape in his face.

The woman was as obstinate as her father, Brandon thought with a curse. He couldn't sit in one of the half-dozen chairs in the small waiting area. He paced.

Fortunately, Anna appeared in only a few minutes, a small bandage on her temple. "She said I'm fine, just as I told you." She glanced back. "I liked her. Didn't you say her father was a real curmudgeon?"

He laughed, letting out the breath he'd been holding. Anna was fine. "Taylor has his bedside manner."

"She was very nice to me," Anna said. "She was telling me she might stay here in Antelope Flats and continue her father's work in infertility." Anna cocked her head at him. "Maybe it's just you she doesn't like," she joked.

Brandon glanced back. Dr. Taylor Ivers watched them leave, a frown on her face. He figured it was for him. Anna might have something there. The woman certainly didn't seem to like him.

Brandon drove back to the marina. The small fishing boat she'd rented was tied up at the dock. She didn't see any of her father's men waiting for them as they climbed into the boat and started across the lake in the darkness.

The lake was quiet. Lights glittered along the shore. Campfires flared from in the pines, and she could smell the smoke and the water. She heard the murmur of voices around the campfires and music carrying on the summer night air, the sound broken only occasionally by laughter.

They were both silent on the ride across the lake, both lost in their own thoughts. Brandon pulled into the dock in front of the dark cabin, tied up the boat and led the way up to the porch.

"Let me make sure we don't have any company," he said, and left her on the porch to go inside.

A few moments later, several lights came on inside and the door opened. She looked at him framed in the doorway and threw herself into his arms—just as she had wanted to do all day.

He cupped her face in his hands and dropped his mouth to hers again.

She sighed as he deepened the kiss, her arms wrapping around his neck, her lips parting in response to the heat of his kisses. "Brand," she whispered against his hot eager mouth. "Make love to me."

Brandon pulled back to look at her. The sounds of the warm summer night wafted around them. She smiled. "Yes," she whispered. "Please."

He laughed softly and kissed her with the longing that had been building up inside him all day. Then he swung her up into his arms as he carried her inside.

She tossed his hat aside and kissed him as he worked his denim jacket off and tossed it onto the floor. Her kisses were teasing, her fingers tangled in hair at the base of his neck as he worked her jacket off.

She slowly began to unbutton her shirt. He watched, mesmerized. The fabric fell open, exposing skin that had never seen the sun. Her white breasts rose and fell with each breath, the dark peaks hard against the silk of her bra.

She grasped the front clasp with both hands and in one swift movement, the bra parted and her breasts were free.

He pulled her to him, his thumbs flicking over the already hard nipples. She let out a groan and pressed against him as he cupped her wonderful breasts in both hands, bending to kiss the rosy tips.

She slithered out of her boots and jeans as he suckled one breast, then the other. She moaned, her head back, her silken white neck exposed.

He kissed her, caught up in the glorious feel of her body, her mouth, her long dark hair tangled in his fingers as her fingers worked the buttons on his shirt, then his jeans.

When he lifted his lips from hers, they were both naked. He held her at arm's length to look at her, soaking up every inch of her luxurious body with his gaze. Goose bumps rippled over her skin, her eyes radiating desire.

She pulled him to the floor, to the bed of clothing and jackets.

His skin was wonderfully browned from working on the ranch without his shirt, his shoulders muscled, his arms strong and well-shaped just like his slim waist and hips.

She trembled as he drew her against him. Her skin felt on fire, his touch a flame that burned across her, setting her center ablaze. She'd dreamed about this moment, but never in her wildest imagination had it been this amazing.

He touched her face as he lay beside her on

the floor, his fingers trailing from her cheek, down her throat to her breasts, his gaze locked with hers. His fingertips moved across the plain of her stomach.

She could feel the heat radiating off his body. His masculine scent filled her. He let out a low chuckle as if he knew he had her cornered. The sound reverberated in her chest, making her heart pound a little faster.

She closed her eyes as his fingers found her center. He gently spread her thighs. She caught her breath, then let it out in a pleasured sigh as he made love to her.

Her senses rose with each touch, each caress, until she was soaring higher and higher. He leaned over her and she looked into his face. She trusted Brandon McCall with her life. But with her love?

She met his pale blue eyes and at that moment she knew she was about to surrender her heart to him, as well. That surrender came with no promises. She knew he didn't believe they stood a chance in hell of being together. She might never be able to change his mind.

"Anna?" he whispered.

She smiled up at him, wrapping her arms around him as he gently filled her. She stared into his eyes, matching his wonderful rhythm as he took her higher and higher until she thought she couldn't stand any more. And then he released her.

She cried out, the pleasure so intense, her body quaked under his. He wrapped her in his arms and kissed away the wetness on her cheeks, smiling down at her. She hadn't even realized that she'd been crying.

It took a few minutes to catch her breath. During that time, he gazed down at her as if memorizing her face.

"I used to dream about what it would be like to kiss you," she said, feeling suddenly shy. "I never dreamed..." She sighed. "Brand."

He kissed her, curling against her on the floor. "We could go to the bed," he whispered.

She laughed. "I'm sure we will. At some point."

And she fell asleep in his arms, as if that day on the curb, when they'd shared the cherry Popsicle, they'd also shared this destiny.

BRANDON WOKE, shocked to see that it was early afternoon. He was starved and tried to remember the last time he'd eaten. They'd picked up a couple of burgers on the way to Brookside. That had been almost a whole day ago. No wonder his stomach was growling.

He rolled over in the double bed and looked at Anna. He couldn't believe they'd slept so late, but then they'd been up half the night making love and talking.

He stared at her. Last night in her arms, he thought everything had changed. But as he looked at her, he knew nothing had. They'd been kidding themselves. They'd needed each other. Fear did that to people. When she opened her eyes this morning, she would see that he was right.

It was time to go to Cash, to tell him everything, to let the law handle this. It was time for Anna to go back to Virginia and the career she obviously loved. He would be on his way to law school in the fall.

Her face was soft in the warm summer light. She looked like an angel, her dark hair spread out around her face. Even knowing how foolish it was, he wanted desperately to kiss her.

Don't fall for this woman, he warned himself as he slipped from the bed and followed the trail of dropped clothing, picking up each piece until, by the time he reached the living room, he was dressed. He checked Anna again to make sure she was still asleep, then closed her door. He would run across the lake to the store by boat and be back before she even knew he was gone. He might even have time to stop by the sheriff's office.

But if he did that without her, he would feel like he was betraying her.

He glanced out the window and saw children already splashing at the edge of the water. Opening the door, he heard the hum of boat motors. The air smelled of pine and water; summer smells. He breathed it in, remembering last night and Anna in his arms. He'd never felt so close to anyone before in his life.

He started down the steps when he saw movement off to his right. An instant later, he felt the pinprick of the needle in his arm. He tried to turn, tried to fight off the men who caught him before he hit the ground. Their faces were the last thing he saw before darkness. VanHorn's men.

ANNA WOKE to a sound. She opened her eyes, forgetting for a moment where she was. With a rush, she remembered the lake cabin—and Brandon. She smiled and started to close her eyes when she realized that the spot next to her on the bed was empty.

"Brand?"

No answer. She sat up. "Brand?"

Maybe he was out on the porch. Or down by the lake.

She got up, drawing the blanket around her as she walked into the living room and stopped cold.

A large redheaded man was sitting in a chair by the window. From his reaction, he'd been waiting for her to wake up. She'd never seen him before, but she knew from the look of him why he was here.

"My name's Red. Get dressed. Your father wants to see you."

"Where is Brandon?"

"You should ask your father about that."

She picked up her clothing, keeping an eye on the man. He watched her, his face expressionless, as she backed into the bathroom with her clothing in hand and shut and locked the door.

The window over the tub was too small even if she'd wanted to escape. But she was ready to face her father. She had to. He had Brandon. Turning on the shower, she stepped under the spray, trying not to think of what her father might have done to him. She had to stay strong. Her father could smell weakness.

For years, she'd let Mason VanHorn feed her lies. Worse, he'd kept her from the ranch she loved. She hadn't put up a fight.

Now he had Brandon.

Her father didn't know it yet, but he was in for the fight of his life.

She showered, dried and dressed quickly, berating herself for not realizing that Mason Van-Horn would use every resource available to him to find her. And his resources were many. She'd known they weren't safe, wouldn't be safe until this was over.

Stepping out of the bedroom, she looked to the large redheaded man still seated where she'd left him.

"I'm ready. Take me to my father."

BRANDON WOKE with a headache and a horrible taste in his mouth. His arm ached where the needle had gone in. He wondered what they'd given him.

Opening his eyes, he blinked in the cool darkness, disoriented and still feeling the effects of the drug.

He pushed himself up, his eyes slowly adjusting to the lack of light. He was in a small old building of some kind—four rough-hewn log walls, a heavy wooden door, no windows.

Anna. Where was Anna?

Stumbling to his feet, he lumbered to the door and tried to open it, not surprised to find it barred from the outside. He leaned against it, waiting for the nausea to pass, then slammed his shoulder into it. The door didn't budge. He cursed under his breath as he rubbed his aching shoulder and listened.

A little light leaked through the cracks in the logs. He leaned against the wall and started to check his watch, but it was gone. How long had he been here?

Pressing his eye to one of the wider cracks, he peered out, surprised at how dark it was. He found a wider crack and peered out, trying to figure out where he was.

It was afternoon, but not as late as he'd first thought. Dark clouds hunkered on the horizon, making it seem later. A thunderstorm was headed this way.

He couldn't see much through the crack in the wall. Just the corner of another building, but he recognized the red-and-white barn. He was on the VanHorn Ranch.

His head began to clear.

He'd known it had been VanHorn's men who abducted him but he hadn't expected them to bring him to the ranch. Why had they? He would have thought they'd have taken him to Mason. Or taken him out somewhere and either shot him or just dumped him.

Instead, he'd been put here as if on hold. What were they waiting for?

In an instant, he knew.

Anna. VanHorn had Anna.

He slammed into the door again with the same result as the first time. Swearing, he looked around the shed. He had to get out of here. Anna was with a monster. There was no telling what the man might do to her. It didn't matter that she was his flesh and blood, his only daughter. Look how he'd treated her all these years. And now she was on to him—and he knew it.

MASON VANHORN was waiting for her in his office. "Thank you, Red," he said without even looking up at them from his desk.

Red left, closing the door behind him and she was alone with her father. "What have you done with Brandon?"

He lifted his head slowly.

For a moment, she was too stunned to speak, amazed at how much he'd aged. She'd always remembered him as being big and powerful, his hair black like her own, his face tanned and strong.

His hair was almost completely white now, his face sallow and lined, but it was his eyes that made her wince. They were dull and dark, lifeless.

She had wanted to see this man suffer, had

come all the way out here to make sure that happened. But one look at him told her he already had suffered more than he ever would at her hands.

"Please sit down."

She shook her head and remained standing.

"I have no idea where McCall is," he said.

"You're lying."

His eyes darkened. "Brandon sold you out," he said quietly. "He went back to his family. He doesn't want any part of this."

She shook her head. "He wouldn't do that." She hated the lack of conviction she heard in her voice. Wasn't that her greatest fear? That she could be wrong about him? Just as she had been about her father?

"Wouldn't he? Then where is he?"

She stared at her father. "I know you did something to him. If you hurt him—"

"Don't be ridiculous," he snapped. "You act as if I had him killed."

"Isn't it easier after the first time?"

He let out a heavy sigh. "Chrissy, what are you doing?"

"Don't call me that. My name is Anna now. Anna Austin."

"You changed your name just to hurt me?"

She laughed but the sound held no humor.

"Everything is about you, isn't it? Why did you have me brought here?"

"I don't understand your anger at me," he said, sounding genuinely confused. "What have I done to you?"

"Give it some thought. It will come to you."

Mason wagged his head sadly. "McCall put you up to this. He's the one feeding you these lies."

"McCall? I should have known you'd blame him. He tried to stop me from finding out the truth about you. I knew this would be a waste of time. All you're going to do is lie to me again. Well, save your breath. I don't believe anything you tell me because I know what happened to my mother. I have proof you put her in Brookside."

All the color drained from his face as he reared back as if she'd slapped him.

"I know you put her in there to punish her. I know what a heartless bastard you really are."

He rose from his chair and started toward her.

Her heart lunged in her chest. She couldn't help but step back, the look in his eyes terrifying her.

He stopped as if shocked. His face seemed to crumble. "Chrissy, I wouldn't hurt you. You can't believe that I would hurt you."

The ridiculousness of his words struck her as funny. She let out the breath she'd been holding. It came out on a laugh. "You killed my little brother or sister, then sent my mother to an insane asylum because she cheated on you. And you don't understand why I'm afraid of you?"

He stared at her, his face a mask of white. "Where would you get the idea…"

"Sarah Gilcrest, my nanny. She heard it all from the room upstairs."

He stumbled back, dropping into the chair behind his desk. He seemed small and she wondered why she'd been afraid of this man only a moment ago. "I don't know what she told you—"

"*She* told me the truth. She heard the baby cry. It wasn't stillborn. She heard my mother begging you not to put her in that place. She heard the doctor take my mother away."

He shook his lowered head without looking at her. "Sarah misunderstood what she heard."

"Like she misunderstood the next morning when you told her the baby was stillborn and my mother had run away?"

He raised his head. "This is why you've done the things you have? Because you believed…" He waved a hand weakly through the air. "Oh, Chrissy— Anna," he corrected. "I see that I should have told you the truth years ago. I swear on everything I hold dear that isn't what happened."

"Everything you hold dear?"

"You hate me." He seemed surprised by that.

"I don't know you," she snapped. "You sent me away when I was ten. I begged you to let me stay here...." Her voice broke. She looked away, hating the tears that burned in her eyes. She would not cry.

"I was trying to protect you."

"Or protect yourself?" she snapped back. "You have a habit of getting rid of things you don't want."

His dark eyes swam in tears. "Is that what you think? That I got rid of you because I didn't want you? Please sit down. I will tell you everything. No more lies."

She knew she couldn't believe him, but she wanted to and that's what frightened her. "I know about Dr. French."

He looked up at her, something in his eyes saying more than she knew his words ever would.

Guilt. She saw the answer. She stumbled back, spinning about to run out the door, out of this house, out of this state. Red stepped into the doorway, his broad chest blocking her escape.

"I can't let you leave until you hear the whole story," her father said flatly.

Anna felt the hair stand up on the back of her neck as she turned to look at him. His expression told her he meant every word.

But once she heard the whole story, what then? He couldn't let her go. He had to know she would go to the sheriff. He couldn't let either her or Brandon go. He had too much to lose.

THERE WAS NO WAY to break down the door, Brandon realized as he looked around the empty space. Nothing to use as a battering ram and he wasn't foolish enough to try again with his shoulder.

The walls were thick square logs. He doubted dynamite could blow through one of them.

He looked up and saw what looked like dim light coming through a corner of the roof. He moved closer. The roof appeared to be the original—only single-thickness sheets of wood nailed across the rafters.

Unless his eyes were playing tricks on him, one corner of the roof had leaked, the wood rotting enough to let in a little light.

The rotten corner was a good ten feet above his head, though, and there was nothing to stand on to reach it.

He looked around for a spot where the chinking between the logs had worked out and climbed up into the open rafters. Clinging precariously from one of the rafters, he swung back and forth until he had enough momentum, then he kicked at the corner of the roof. The wood gave a little.

Hope soared through him. He swung again. And again. The wood broke away at the corner. He could see daylight, smell the storm headed this way. Lightning flickered, thunder boomed. The storm just might hide the noise he was making. If only he could make a hole large enough to get out before he was discovered.

Another thunderous boom overhead. He stopped for a moment, his hands burning from swinging on the rafter, his legs aching. Just a little more.

He heard the crunch of footsteps. Someone tried the door.

"PLEASE, SIT DOWN," Mason VanHorn said, motioning to a chair. "Red, would you close the door?"

Anna pulled the chair to her, putting as much distance as she could between them. Her father saw the movement, knew what she was doing. The pain in his expression gave her no pleasure. He was holding her here against her will.

Just as she knew he was holding Brandon. She just prayed he hadn't hurt him.

"Your mother was never strong."

She told herself she wouldn't believe anything he told her but the moment he started to speak, something in his voice told her she was finally about to hear the truth.

"It started before—" he waved a hand through the air "—before her affair, before her pregnancy. Then, when the baby was born… The baby was horribly deformed. When your mother saw it, she just…lost her mind."

"What did you do with the baby?"

"The doctor wrapped him in a towel—" His voice broke. "I couldn't bear to look…."

"You didn't see him?" Anna asked.

He shook his head. "I took him out and buried him in the VanHorn graveyard on the hill. At the very last moment I parted the towel and looked into his face. He was beautiful. Just like your mother."

As hard as she tried not to, she started to cry.

"Helena had been hanging on to reality by a thread. After that…" He looked down at his hands. They were weathered and covered with age spots. The hands of an old man. "She fought me, throwing everything she could get her hands on. I tried to console her but she…"

He shook his head and she saw that he was crying.

Anna had never seen her father cry. It was a shocking sight. She didn't want to have any sympathy for him. "How can I believe you?"

He didn't seem to hear her. "She'd been seeing Dr. French. For her…problems. That night…there was nothing I could do. I couldn't let you and Holt see her like that. I was afraid that she might…" He looked up and she saw the fear in his face. He thought she might hurt her other children? "Dr. French took her to Brookside."

Anna sat motionless. "How long was she at Brookside?" she asked into the silence that followed.

"Until she died. When you were nine."

Anna had known her mother had to be dead but still, it hit her hard. She was too stunned to speak for a moment. "That's why you sent me away?"

"I wanted to protect you."

"Does my brother know?"

"Holt?" He shook his head.

"Why did you lie all these years?" But the moment the words were out of her mouth, she knew. "The baby was alive at birth, just like Sarah said. You had the doctor kill it."

AT THE SOUND of someone at the door, Brandon froze, hanging from the rafter. An engine fired up nearby. He used the sudden noise to cloak the sound of his boots hitting the floor as he dropped down and curled back up on the floor.

He heard the lock click. The door opened a crack. Someone called out. A truck door slammed. The door closed and whoever had opened it locked the door again and moved away, his footfalls retreating. The truck motor revved and then there was silence again.

Climbing back up the log wall, Brandon grabbed the rafter and kicked again at the roof, praying he could get out of here and to Anna before it was too late. Unless someone had just taken her away in that truck.

The roof splintered under his boot, the hole large enough that he should be able to wriggle through.

Climbing across to the end rafter, he reached an arm out and grabbed the corner of the overhang. Holding on, he shoved his shoulder and head through the hole, then worked his other shoulder out.

Bracing himself with both hands on the remaining roof, he pushed upward until he was sitting on the roof.

He could see the ranch complex up the road.

Mason VanHorn's car was parked in front of the ranch house.

Jumping down, Brandon ran along the back side of the buildings, headed for the ranch house. If anyone knew where Anna was, it was Mason VanHorn.

"ANNA, YOU HAVE TO understand—"

She was on her feet again. "You were covering up a murder."

"I didn't kill that baby. He was so badly deformed that he only lived a few moments."

"Then why lie?"

Her father rose from the chair but didn't come toward her. Instead, he moved to the window at the rear of his office and stood with his back to her. "I am ashamed, but the truth is I couldn't bear for anyone to know about your mother. I didn't want her…sickness to make people in town treat you and Holt differently. There is so much about mental illness that we don't understand. It was worse thirty years ago."

"You shut her away in that place because you were embarrassed?"

He turned to look at her. "You don't understand. She was violent. She—" His eyes filled again with tears—and a look that froze her blood with horror.

"No," Anna cried. "My mother killed the baby!"

Chapter Thirteen

Cash put down the twenty-year-old Jane Doe murder file next to his notes on the Emma Ingles murder.

He could find no connection. Not that he'd expected to find one.

But he'd discovered when he talked to the motel clerk where Lenore Johnson had been staying that his brother Brandon had been asking about her, too. Lenore had also asked for directions to Brookside the last night she was seen.

Cash had been trying without any luck to find his little brother. He couldn't wait to ask him what he'd been doing at Brookside with Frank Yarrow and why he'd let the Realtor believe the McCall family might be interested in buying the place.

Brandon was also seen with a dark-haired young woman.

Yep. Cash couldn't wait to get his hands on his brother. Whatever Brandon was up to, he just hoped it had nothing to do with Emma Ingles's murder.

Molly had called earlier and was holding dinner for him. Just the thought of her made him close the file and reach to turn out his light.

The phone rang. A 911 call forwarded to his number. He picked it up. "Sheriff Cash McCall."

"Help me. Please help me." The whispering voice of a woman made him sit up straighter. *"My name is Lenore Johnson. I don't have much time before he comes back."* Her words were slurred, he could barely hear her. *"I'm being held at Brookside. I think he's a doctor. He—"*

The line went dead.

"Hello? Hello?"

Cash hung up the phone, his heart pounding. He quickly picked up the receiver again and dialed his home to tell Molly dinner would have to wait.

THE LOCK on the bathroom window behind the VanHorn ranch house was still broken, just as Brandon had suspected. Mason's men either hadn't had time to fix it or had left it hoping to catch the vandal.

Carefully lifting the window, he slipped inside. He could hear voices coming from down the hall.

At the door, he looked out. He hadn't seen any of VanHorn's men. Not even Red. Maybe he'd sent them all off, wanting to be alone with his daughter. The thought chilled Brandon.

The hallway was empty, the door to Van-Horn's office closed. He could hear voices behind the office door. Mason was talking quietly, almost reassuringly.

Brandon moved silently down the hallway and put his ear against the door. He couldn't hear what was being said but it sounded as if Anna was crying and Mason was trying to soothe her.

He knew he would have hell getting Anna out of here without a fight and unfortunately, he had no weapon. Playing hero now could just get them both killed.

But there was no other option. He could call his brother but it would take Cash too long to get here.

He gripped the doorknob, listening.

"ANNA, I'M SO SORRY that I didn't tell you the truth before," Mason said in a monotone, his head down. He looked horrible, as if reliving all this had aged him more.

Anna didn't know what to say. Or what to believe. If he was telling the truth… "What about my mother?"

He raised his head to meet her gaze and she knew at once that she didn't want to hear this. "She's dead."

"You already told me that." She bit her lip. "Where?"

He looked away and she knew he'd had to cover up her death, as well—with Dr. French's help.

She sighed. "So many lies. Was it worth it?"

A spark lit in his dark eyes. "To protect you and your brother? Yes. I would do it all over again."

She stared at him. How much of it had been for her and Holt? And how much for her father? "Who was the man?" she asked, thinking about the feud between her father and Asa.

He shook his head. "Just one of many cowboys."

Anna felt sick. "She died at Brookside?"

"Twenty years ago."

That long? She knew she should feel relieved that her mother hadn't suffered for years in that place.

"She was starting to get better," Mason said. "She knew who I was and she even asked about you and Holt." His voice broke.

The phone rang. He jumped as if it were a rattlesnake on his desk. It rang again. He seemed to be trying to ignore it and something in his expression made her suspicious.

"Go head, answer it," she said as it rang again. "Isn't that your private line?"

It rang again. Clearly, he wasn't going to answer it.

Before he could stop her, she stood, reached over and picked up the phone. All she wanted was to see who was calling, to verify her hunch on the caller ID.

"Dr. French's number." She hit Talk but said nothing, her gaze going to her father's.

The answering machine started to pick up. "Mason, it's Niles. I know you're there. You have to get up to Brookside. You have to stop—"

Her father grabbed the phone from her before French could finish.

Anna stumbled backward toward the door, tears burning her eyes. "It was all a lie, wasn't it?"

"No," Mason cried. "I told you the honest-to-God truth. You have to believe me."

She was shaking her head, moving away from him, wanting to run. For a while there, she'd believed him. "Where is the private investigator I hired? What did you do with her? Is that why you have to get up to Brookside? Who is it you have to stop? Lenore Johnson, the woman I hired? Or me?"

"Chrissy, listen to me." He slammed down the phone and grabbed her arm. She tried to break free.

She heard a sound behind her and spun around to see Brandon framed in the doorway.

"Let her go," Brandon ordered, and reached for her.

"I could have you arrested," Mason snapped at Brandon, but he let go of Anna. She grabbed up the set of keys from her father's desk, the keys to his SUV.

Brandon pulled her to him, drawing her close, his arm around her as they backed out of the room. "Don't try to stop us."

"Chrissy, if you leave here, I can't protect you. I'm afraid of what Dr. French will do once he knows that I told you everything."

BRANDON PUT HIMSELF between Mason Van-Horn and his daughter. "I'm taking her to Cash," he said. "I've already called him. He knows that you had me abducted. He knows Anna is here. If I don't call him back soon, he will come out here with the state police." It was all a lie, but one that seemed to be working.

VanHorn stumbled back, dropping into his chair, his face slack with defeat.

"She'll be safe with the sheriff," Brandon said. "It's over."

"Yes," he said, not looking at either of them as they left.

Brandon rushed Anna out the front door to her father's expensive SUV parked outside. She slid into the passenger seat as he swung behind the wheel and started the motor.

He'd expected Mason to send out an alert to his men but as Brandon spun the SUV around and headed down the ranch road, he didn't see anyone coming after them.

"Are you all right?" he asked, putting his arm around her and pulling her closer. One look at her face told him she was far from all right.

When he reached the highway, he headed toward Antelope Flats. The thunderstorm raced across the landscape, clouds low and dark, lightning flickering and thunder a drum in the distance.

She filled him in, including Dr. French's phone call.

"I lied about calling Cash, but I have to now," he said to Anna, afraid she might want to argue.

She didn't. She nodded, still looking numb, her face pale.

He stopped at the phone booth in front of the Decker Post Office. Decker, Montana, consisted of the post office and a couple of houses. At one time, there'd been a bar but it had closed years ago.

"I'll be right back." He got out and stepped into the phone booth as the first drops of rain began to fall. They pelted the phone booth. Brandon looked through them to the empty highway, afraid Mason would have a bunch of his cowboys hot on their trail.

"Brandon?" Cash said the moment he came on the line. "What the hell is going on? Frank Yarrow called me wanting to know if my family was still interested in buying Brookside. He said he gave you a tour."

"It's a long story. Where are you?"

"The dispatcher patched you through. I've got a lead on Lenore Johnson."

"At Brookside?" Brandon asked in surprise.

"I'm not sure how you're involved in all this—"

"Cash, Mason VanHorn just got a call from a Dr. French. Something is going on up there. I'll tell you everything when I see you."

"Stay away from Brookside. There have already been two murders—"

"*Two?* I saw the story about Emma Ingles—"

"There was another one twenty years ago in Room 9B."

All the air rushed from Brandon's lungs. "9B? That was Helena VanHorn's room. We'll tell you everything when you get to Brookside." He hung up before his brother could argue.

"*WE'LL* TELL YOU everything? Brandon!" Cash swore as he sped out of town, siren and lights blaring, headed for Brookside, wondering how deeply his brother was involved in this.

Lightning flickered on the horizon as dark clouds swept toward him. He raced down the empty highway in the growing darkness as rain pelted the windshield as hard as gravel. He turned on the wipers as the storm became a downpour and visibility dropped.

Just a few miles outside of town, he saw a set of headlights flash on from a side road. Even with the rain, Cash knew the driver had to see him coming with the lights and siren on.

The next instant, the car pulled out in front of him. He swerved, realizing too late that the driver had pulled out on purpose. The patrol car went into a skid on the wet pavement.

It happened fast. One moment he was on the highway, the next, he was sliding across the pavement, hitting the graveled edge of the road and was airborne.

BRANDON HAD JUST climbed back into the SUV when he saw a set of headlights in his rearview mirror. A vehicle was coming up the highway moving fast. He recognized the rig as it sped past. Red's pickup. Only Red wasn't driving. Mason VanHorn was.

Mason didn't seem to see them, his attention on the highway at the high speed he was traveling.

"That was my father," Anna said, sitting up to stare after him. She looked over at Brandon. "Follow him."

Brandon nodded, pretty sure he knew where VanHorn was headed. The same place Cash was. Brookside.

"I believed him," Anna said as Brandon took off after the pickup. She shook her head. "I actually believed him. Until Dr. French called."

"Cash is on his way to Brookside. He said he had a lead on Lenore Johnson."

"Oh, my God!" Anna cried. "That must be why Dr. French was calling my father, telling him he had to come to Brookside. He said, 'You have to stop—' Stop something. Or someone?"

THE SHERIFF'S DEPARTMENT patrol car slammed down, tires digging into the side of the ditch, and rolled in a shower of mud and rain and weeds.

Cash lost track of time as he crashed down

into the deep ditch beside the highway. He'd lost his sense of direction as the car rolled. He wasn't sure which side was up or down.

Then everything stopped. He hung from his seat belt for a moment in stunned silence. He was alive. The patrol car had landed upside down in the ditch. He'd been wearing his seat belt and the airbag had deployed. Nothing hurt, at least that he could feel.

He unhooked his seat belt and dropped to the roof of the car. For a moment he just lay there, trying to get his bearings. He tried the door. It opened about ten inches before getting stuck in the mud. He reached over and tried the passenger side door. It swung open and he crawled out into the rain and darkness. He couldn't see the other car, only the glow of the headlights above him on the road.

He hadn't hit the other car but he couldn't be sure the other driver hadn't wrecked, as well. Or was the driver just waiting to finish the job he started?

Cash drew his pistol and started up the steep embankment. It was slick and he had to scramble in the wet, loose dirt. He didn't see the man until he was almost on top of him.

At the rim of the embankment, Cash blinked through the rain and saw the large dark figure for just an instant before he saw the gun in the man's hand. The man seemed just as surprised to see him and drew back his boot, kicking at Cash's head.

Cash managed to dodge the worst of the man's kick, catching a glancing blow to the shoulder. But his pistol went flying as he fell backward down the embankment.

A bullet zinged past as he tumbled back to the bottom of the ditch. Scrambling to his feet, he ducked behind the patrol car and reached inside for his shotgun as a shot ricocheted off the roof.

Glancing back up toward the highway, he saw the man silhouetted against the blurred headlights. He hadn't gotten a good look at him at the top of the embankment. Just a feel for the man's size—and intent.

The man hadn't wanted to kill him or he would have shot him—not kicked him when he had the chance. Did that mean he was only trying to detain him? Is that why he was taking potshots at him, trying to hold him down here? Until what? Until someone took care of Lenore Johnson at Brookside?

Cash swore and looked down the road a ways to where the embankment wasn't quite as steep. He waited after a bolt of lightning flashed above the highway for the darkness that followed, and then took off running.

Scrambling up the embankment, he ran to the man's car and hunkered down next to it. The car was a black SUV, some foreign job. The side was scraped, as if the driver had already been in an accident.

The man was still standing at the edge of the embankment looking down. Thunder boomed overhead. Cash saw the man jump back as if he thought he'd been shot at. He turned and started toward his car.

Cash waited until he was close enough, then rose up, pointing the shotgun at the man's chest. "Freeze!"

The man raised his gun and fired a wild shot. Cash pulled the shotgun's trigger. Light flared in the rain. The man dropped to the wet pavement.

Cash moved quickly to him, kicking away the man's weapon before he looked down at his face.

A pair of vacant eyes stared blankly up at him. "Josh Davidson?" Why the hell would the orderly from the clinic run him off the road and try to keep him from getting to Brookside?

BRANDON DROVE the narrow road up the mountain, his headlights cutting a swath through the low dark clouds of the storm. Lightning flashed. Thunder boomed on its heels. He was already jumpy after the last time they'd come up this road. For all he knew, Dr. French or VanHorn might be waiting just around the next corner. Only this time, French or VanHorn might succeed in forcing them over the cliff.

Anna sat staring ahead, her hands clenched in her lap. He could see the fear on her face. What would they find at Brookside? He hated to think.

As he rounded the curve, Brookside rose up like a monster on the dark horizon.

Several large raindrops splattered against the windshield. Brandon jumped, his nerves raw. The rain came hard and fast, blurring everything as he pulled up to the front door—directly behind Red's pickup, which Mason VanHorn had been driving.

The driver's-side door of the pickup was standing open, Mason no longer behind the wheel. Something large and dark moved through the rain, disappearing into the inky black shadow of the building.

There were no other vehicles in the lot. No sign of Cash's patrol car. He should have been here by now. Brandon realized with a start that something had to have happened to keep him from beating them here.

Anna let out a cry. "Did you see that? I saw someone at a window on the third floor."

He looked up through the windshield in the direction she pointed. He saw nothing but darkness.

"I'm going in," Anna said, and reached for her door handle.

"We should wait for Cash," Brandon said beside her.

She looked over at him. "He should have been here by now. Lenore's in there. I can't let him kill her." She opened her door and slipped out. She didn't even feel the rain as she ran toward the front steps.

She wished she had a weapon, anything. But there was little chance for finding something she could use in the rainy darkness. She could hear Brandon behind her, but she didn't look back as she topped the steps and felt her breath catch.

From inside the dark building came the clank of an elevator door opening.

A bolt of lightning cut a brilliant white ragged tear in the sky illuminating Brookside. In that split second of blinding light, she saw that the front doors stood open. Clearly someone had been expected. Her father? Or her and Brandon?

Anna felt Brandon's hand on her arm. He

pointed to the front doors. She could see the worry on his face. It matched her own. But she couldn't wait. She had to go inside. Her father was in there. With Dr. French? And what about Lenore?

Anna had gotten the woman into this. She had to help her. If it wasn't too late.

She stepped through the double doors into the entryway. The cold silence of the building settled over her. The office was dark. So was the hallway past it. Her gaze fell to the worn linoleum floor. Wet footprints.

The footprints were headed in the opposite direction—not toward the office corridor—but toward the wing for the criminally insane.

"Wait," Brandon whispered next to her.

She turned to watch him go into the office. He came back out with a large heavy-duty flashlight. He flicked it on. The battery was low, the light dim. He shone it down the hallway past the office. Empty.

When he shone it the other way, the light caught the wet footprints before shining on the open double doors of the wing that had once housed the violent, the criminally insane. Her mother, Anna thought with a horrible jolt. The light illuminated the number on the door of 9B.

Past it, the corridor was pitch-black. She

thought she heard footfalls somewhere in the building, the echo making it hard to determine from where. But all her instincts told her that the figure she'd seen in the third-floor window was now on this floor.

She started in that direction when she heard a door open behind her and the creak of a sole on the floor. She spun around as a slight dark figure came stumbling out of the ladies' restroom, a piece of galvanized pipe clutched in both hands. Even as dark as it was, Anna could see that the woman's eyes were wild and she was breathing hard.

Brandon started to launch himself at the woman. "It's Lenore!" Anna cried.

Lenore only got a few steps before her legs gave out under her. Brandon caught her before she hit the floor, gently laying her down and prying the pipe from her fingers.

"It's all right," he whispered, and glanced at Anna. "She looks like she's been drugged."

"Have…been…drugged," Lenore slurred and tried to focus her gaze as Anna knelt beside her.

"Lenore, it's me, Anna Austin. You're all right now. You're safe."

Lenore shook her head. "Dr. French…" She closed her eyes, licked her lips and whispered, "Still here."

Anna looked down the hallway in the direction from which Lenore had come, then shifted her gaze to the wet footprints. They had to be her father's. Then where was Dr. French?

Anna picked up the pipe Brandon had taken from Lenore and the flashlight. She rose and shone the light in the direction of 9B. The wet footprints glistened in the light. She moved toward the wing for the criminally insane.

"Anna, wait. Don't."

She barely heard Brandon's words.

The chain was no longer on the doors to the wing, but hanging down, the padlock on the floor.

She stepped through the doors. Ahead, the wet footprints disappeared at Room 9B. The flashlight went out. She shook it. The light flickered on. She stepped to the open door of 9B. The flashlight went out again.

She stopped, swallowed back the fear that made her palms damp, her heart a thunderous ache in her chest, and took a step into the dark room. Her ankle brushed up against something. Her heart stopped.

She shook the flashlight. The light flickered on and she let out a cry as she stared at the body at her feet.

CASH HAD no choice. He rolled Josh Davidson's body off the road and, taking the man's keys, ran to the SUV.

Because of the isolation in this part of the state, Cash didn't have a full-time deputy. Didn't really need one. The few instances he'd needed help, he'd call the state investigators in Billings and they'd sent down someone.

Unfortunately, Billings was two hours away. No time for anyone to drive down. He was on his own.

The front of the vehicle had been badly crushed. One headlight was cocked at an odd angle. What the hell had Davidson hit? Cash didn't want to think.

He leaped behind the wheel and started the car, glad to hear the engine turn over on the first try. He didn't know how much time he'd lost. His greatest fear was that Brandon would reach Brookside before he did. Lenore's call scared him. Someone had been holding her at the old mental institution. But what scared him the most was the way her call had been cut off.

The rain fell harder, the sky was even darker, as he turned onto the dirt road to Brookside. There were other tracks. Brandon's. But also several other vehicles'. Cash swore and gave the SUV more gas, fear driving him up the mountainside.

He just prayed it wasn't too late.

ANNA HEARD Brandon's running footfalls behind her. She turned away from the body on the floor.

Brandon took the flashlight from her. "Oh, God," he said as he shone the light on the body.

Out of the corner of her eye, she watched him kneel down to check for a pulse. "He's still warm. He hasn't been dead long."

Anna looked again at the body, unable to hide her shock. "It's Dr. French," she said, her voice coming out in a hoarse whisper. But how could that be? If he was the killer… His eyes bulged, his face was blue, a rope was tied so tightly around his neck that it cut into his flesh. There were horrible scratches on his throat where he'd fought to tear the rope away to no avail.

"My father killed him," Anna cried.

Brandon put his arms around Anna. She pressed her face to his chest. "Let's get out of here, okay?"

Lenore had joined them. She stumbled up and leaned against the door for support. "We have to get out before he comes back." Her eyelids were heavy and it looked as if it took everything in her to stay on her feet.

Brandon released Anna to shine the flashlight on the body. "Dr. French is dead. He won't be coming back."

Lenore looked down at the body lying just inside Room 9B. She blinked as if trying to focus. "That's not him."

Brandon exchanged a look with Anna. "This isn't the man who locked you up here?"

Lenore shook her head.

"But that's Dr. French," Anna said.

"I might be higher than a kite but I know the face of the bastard who did this to me," Lenore spat. "He said to call him Dr. French…but that isn't the man. The other one must have killed him."

"The other one?" Brandon asked, afraid of what Lenore was going to say. If Anna was right and her father had killed Dr. French—

"He must have lied about his name," Lenore said and turned to look behind her. "That's the man."

They all turned to see the tall man in the dark coat standing in the dim hallway behind them holding the gun.

"I'll take that flashlight," Dr. Ivers said. "And

please put down that pipe, Ms. VanHorn. We've had quite enough drama for one night."

The authority and calmness in his tone sent a chill through Brandon as he handed over the flashlight, the light shining on the floor at their feet.

Brandon shot Anna a look. Her face was ghostlike in the eerie light, but she looked strangely calm as she dropped the length of pipe to the floor.

It clattered at her feet. "So if you aren't Dr. French, then who are you?" Lenore Johnson asked.

"Dr. Ivers," he said as he pushed them back toward the door to the room. He stooped, keeping the gun trained on Brandon, to pick up the pipe. "I have been known to use Dr. French's name, though, when the need arose." He motioned with the gun for them to step back into Room 9B. "If you would, please."

He sounded exactly as he always had at the clinic, all the years he'd stitched up Brandon and his brothers.

"What the hell is going on?" Brandon asked.

Dr. Ivers gave him a look that said he didn't like swearing. Or being talked back to. "I think you're smart enough to figure out that

I'm going to lock you in that room for a while."

"Why?" Brandon asked, seeing something in the elderly doctor's eyes that frightened him more than the gun.

Ivers sighed. "Please don't be difficult, Brandon. I tired of you and your brothers' antics long ago."

"You can't keep us all locked up here," Lenore said. "Give it up, old man. It's over. Whatever it is that you're trying to hide, the cat is out of the bag."

Anna had been watching the doctor, trying to understand how Dr. French could be dead, why the kindly Dr. Ivers had pretended to be French and, more important, why he was now holding a gun on them.

Then she knew. "You delivered my mother's baby," she said. "That's what this is about, isn't it? My father let me believe Dr. French must have delivered the baby."

He smiled forlornly. "Your father used to tell me what a bright girl you were. He was always bragging about your articles, all those awards for investigative journalism. He was so proud of you. What a shame you had to use all that skill to try to destroy so many lives."

"This is more than covering up a baby's

death," Anna said. "Or my mother's confinement here. You and my father made some kind of deal. Why else would you go along with it otherwise?"

Dr. Ivers looked over his shoulder. Was he expecting someone? "Why couldn't you have just left it alone?" he demanded. "My wife of sixty-two years is very sick. She doesn't have much time left. I won't have her distraught by all this. Do you understand?"

"Distraught, my ass," Lenore said. "You kill us and I promise your wife will be more than distraught when she finds out."

"My Emily only has a few days left," he said.

"What about your daughter?" Brandon asked. "Taylor."

"My daughter, yes." He glanced over at Anna. "I won't be able to protect Taylor. But I can at least spare my wife any further pain. I owe her that much."

"Don't you at least owe *me* the truth?" Anna said. "You delivered my little brother. What happened to him?"

"He was stillborn, just as your father told you."

She shook her head. "My nanny heard the baby cry. Did my mother kill the baby?" she asked with a sob.

Dr. Ivers furrowed his brows. He seemed distracted and she could tell he was listening for something. A vehicle? "Your father had feared she would. I let him believe she had. Your father was already so upset, he would have believed anything I told him but the baby was stillborn just as I said. I sent him off to bury it."

That moment of hesitation. "The nanny *heard* a baby cry."

Dr. Ivers looked startled as if her words had finally sunk in.

"The nanny was in the room right upstairs." Anna let out a gasp at a sudden realization. "There had to have been *another* baby. Twins. That's why you told my mother to stay in bed during the pregnancy."

"Enough," Dr. Ivers snapped. "Step into the room."

"No. Tell me the truth. There was another baby, wasn't there? What did you do with it?"

Brandon swore. "He kept it. Earlier at the clinic when I saw you and Taylor together I thought how much—"

"I don't want to shoot any of you, but I will if I have to," Dr. Ivers said, suddenly agitated. "All of you into the room."

"Taylor is my *sister?*" Anna cried. She remembered the competent doctor at the clinic who'd bandaged her head. The woman had dark hair and eyes like Anna's mother. Like Anna. Taylor, the only child of elderly parents.

Anna heard a car coming up the road, the whine of the engine a faint buzz. Cash? Was it the sheriff?

Or was it someone else? Whoever Dr. Ivers was expecting?

The doctor tilted his head. He heard the sound, too. "Time is up." He pulled the trigger. The report echoed like a cannon through the hallway. The bullet lodged in the padding in Room 9B.

Anna jumped back.

"I'm not going back in that room," Lenore said, standing her ground. "You can just shoot me."

"Have it your way," Dr. Ivers said and pointed the gun at her.

Brandon stepped in front of the private investigator. "You don't want to kill anyone. Think of Taylor. She is going to have to live with whatever you do here today."

Dr. Ivers shoved Brandon backward, knocking Lenore back, as well. Lenore stumbled over Dr. French's body and started to fall. Anna caught her. The doctor reached to close the door.

Anna saw movement behind him. Her father. He staggered up behind Dr. Ivers, his white hair wet from the rain, his expression pained. Blood ran down one side of his face. He had a gun in his hand. He pointed it unsteadily at the doctor's back.

"I can't let you do that," Mason VanHorn said. "It's over, Doc. It's finally over."

"Sorry, Mason, but this time I hold all the cards." Dr. Ivers swung around, leading with the pipe her father couldn't have seen in Ivers's hand.

"No!" Anna yelled as the pipe struck the gun in her father's hand and sent it skittering across the worn tile floor.

Dr. Ivers pulled the trigger. Anna saw her father stagger backward and fall. Before the doctor could get off another shot, Brandon hit Ivers from behind. Ivers stumbled forward, fell toward the opposite wall, caught himself and then kept going down the corridor at a run.

"Get him!" Lenore cried. "The bastard is getting away."

But Anna could have cared less about Dr. Ivers. She ran to her father and knelt beside him. His shoulder bloomed red with blood. She hurriedly stripped off her jacket and put it on the wound. His eyes were closed. She quickly checked his pulse. It was faint.

"Brandon, get help!" she cried. "We have to get him to the hospital."

"Ivers won't get far," Brandon assured Lenore as a vehicle pulled up out front; a car door slammed. He ran down the hall and called back to them, "It's Cash." Turning to his brother, he cried, "Call 911."

Chapter Fourteen

"Your old man saved our lives," Lenore said, sitting down next to Anna on the floor as they waited for the ambulance. "Go figure."

Anna held her jacket to his wound, clutching his hand with her free one. "You're going to make it," she whispered. "Damn you, don't you leave me now."

Brandon put his arm around her. They could hear the sound of the ambulance siren in the distance.

Cash waited for the ambulance. As the attendants loaded Mason into the back of the ambulance, he asked Brandon, "I'm going after Dr. Ivers. Where will you be?"

"With Anna. Christianna VanHorn. At the hospital."

Cash looked at Anna standing next to Brandon. "So you're Christianna VanHorn." He glanced at his brother, a questioning look that said he was going to be demanding some answers. "I'll want to talk to you both. You'd better take Ms. Johnson to the hospital with you. Who knows what the doc had been giving her drugwise."

Brandon nodded, his hold on Anna tightening. "I'll take care of them."

Cash smiled and dropped his hand on his brother's shoulder as he left in the familiar-looking black SUV with the dents.

"I wonder what that's about," Brandon said, more to himself than to Anna. She was watching the ambulance pull out. He walked her and Lenore to Mason's SUV and followed the ambulance to the Sheridan hospital.

The doctors admitted Lenore for observation against her protests—and took Mason right into surgery.

"You don't have to stay," Anna said as he waited with her.

"I'd like to. If you want me here," he said.

She nodded, tears in her eyes. He put his arms around her. She leaned into his chest, and they waited several hours until a doctor finally came out to tell them the news.

"He should make it," the young male doctor assured Anna. "He has a slight concussion from a blow to the head and he's lost blood from the head wound and the gunshot but no vital organs were affected. He's strong for his age and in good shape. Now it just comes down to a will to live."

"May I see him?" Anna asked.

"He's sedated. But you can go in for a few minutes."

BRANDON WAITED outside as she went into the room. Her father looked so old against the white of the sheets, his face pale and haggard. She stared down at him for a long time, not knowing what to say.

"I love you. I've always loved you." She touched his weathered hand, remembering how he'd been when she was a girl. If only she could find that man in this one. If only she got the chance.

"Please come with me home to the ranch," Brandon said when she came out of her father's room.

She wiped her tears and looked at him in surprise. "Are you sure they'll want a VanHorn under their roof? Especially after they hear what happened?"

Brandon had been the one who'd said they had no chance because of their families and the feud. "I was wrong," he said. "Come on." He reached for her hand.

She smiled through her tears and took his hand.

At least he hoped to hell he was wrong about their families, because right now he wanted her with him and there was only one place he wanted to be—on the McCall ranch.

CASH DROVE Davidson's SUV up to the front door of Dr. Porter Ivers's house. All the lights were on. Dr. Ivers's car was in the drive. He'd half expected the doc to run. Ivers had had plenty of time. Cash was a good forty-five minutes behind him, but he hadn't been able to leave until the ambulance got up the road and he was sure the others were safe.

Cash was worried. He didn't have the whole story yet. Brandon had filled him in on some of it, but Cash still had three unsolved murders— Emma Ingles, Dr. Niles French and Helena Van-Horn, the Jane Doe in Room 9B at Brookside.

All Cash knew at this point was that Dr. Ivers had shot Mason VanHorn, held Lenore Johnson captive and threatened his brother and Christianna VanHorn.

That was enough to pick him up and arrest him until all of this could be sorted out.

He didn't see Taylor Ivers's car and wondered if she was still at the clinic—or if her father had taken her car. Cash climbed out of the

SUV, weapon drawn, and approached the house.

Dr. Porter Ivers lived in one of the large old homes in Antelope Flats. He'd come here right after he'd married his wife Emily and took over the clinic after Dr. Neibauer retired.

Cash recalled talk around town that Dr. Ivers and his wife had hoped to fill that huge old house with children. When Emily couldn't get pregnant, the doctor had become interested in infertility.

He'd helped other infertile couples, including Leticia Arnold's parents, have children. At least that had been what Cash had believed.

But as Cash walked up the steps to the front door, he had a bad feeling about how the doctor had "delivered" those babies.

The door was standing open. He looked through the screen into the lit living room. Everything was neat. No sign of anyone, or anything out of place. No sounds at all.

He knocked on the door frame, waited and knocked a little louder. He couldn't help but remember walking by this house on a summer evening and seeing Doc and Emily sitting on the porch trying to catch a cool breeze. No one who'd seen them together would ever doubt the devotion they had for each other.

Cash knocked again. No answer. A bad feeling settled over him as he pushed open the screen door and stepped inside.

"Dr. Ivers. It's Sheriff Cash McCall. Please come down."

No answer.

He checked the lower rooms, then started up the stairs, afraid of what he would find.

BRANDON DROVE home to the Sundown Ranch through the growing darkness. The lights were on inside the ranch house as he parked out front and glanced at his watch, surprised it was only eight-thirty. It felt like midnight.

He opened his door and Anna slid out after him. He took her hand, felt the tension in her. She was the one who said it didn't matter how their families felt about them being together. She'd lied and now he knew it.

"It's going to be all right," he tried to assure her.

She gave him a look that said she highly doubted that.

"Your father is going to get better," he pointed out.

"And go to prison for his crimes, whatever they all are." She shook her head. "I hate to think that you were probably right about our families."

He squeezed her hand. "It doesn't matter."

She smiled up at him sadly. "Yes, it does."

As they started up the steps, the front door opened. Shelby stood framed in the doorway. "Brandon? Who is that with you?" She turned on the porch lights.

"Mother, this is Christianna VanHorn," he said.

Shelby blinked in surprise. Either from the fact that a VanHorn was standing on her porch, or that he'd finally called her Mother.

"I prefer Anna," Anna said.

"Anna." Shelby extended her hand, taking in the dirty, blood-stained jeans. "Come in, please."

Anna let Shelby draw her into the house. Brandon followed. He could forgive his mother everything at that moment. He'd been lying to himself. He was worried as hell what kind of reception they would both get.

Of course, there was still his father. Asa could be a hard, unforgiving man. And while having Shelby back had softened him, he was still a force to contend with sometimes.

"Oh, dear," Shelby said, looking them over once inside the house. "What has happened?"

"It's a long story," Brandon said.

"Have you two eaten?" Shelby asked. "We were just having a late dessert, but I can have

Martha fix you both a plate from dinner. You look like you could use it."

"That would be great," Brandon said.

Anna nodded. "Thank you."

His older brother J.T. came out of the dining room. He seemed surprised to see Brandon with a woman. Brandon realized he'd never brought one home before.

"Come on in and meet the rest of the family," Brandon said, his gaze locking with J.T.'s.

"Anna, would you like to freshen up?" Shelby asked. "There's a powder room right down the hall. Dusty's about your size. I'm sure we can rustle up some clean clothes."

"Thank you," Anna said as she looked down at her jeans. Her fingers went to her father's dried blood on her pant leg.

"Dusty," Shelby called. "Get a pair of your jeans, a blouse and a brush for Anna."

"I should clean up some, too," Brandon said, but he hated to leave Anna down here alone with his family.

"She'll be fine," Shelby said with a fierce motherly look that made him grin. "You don't have to worry about her."

"I'll be right back." As he took the stairs to his room, he heard Shelby giving orders to Martha to set plates for the two of them. Then he heard his mother go into the dining room and announce that Brandon and Christianna Van-Horn would be joining them.

"What the hell?" Asa bellowed before someone closed the dining room door, drowning him out.

When Brandon came back downstairs, Anna was dressed in a pair of his little sister Dusty's dungarees and western shirt. Her hair was brushed, her face no longer smudged with dust.

She smiled as he joined her in the dining room.

His father showed the most surprise as Brandon sat down. Asa started to speak, but Shelby put a hand on his shoulder.

Martha served them both plates heaped with roast beef, mashed potatoes, gravy, fresh corn from the garden and sliced tomatoes.

They ate as Shelby kept a light conversation going. Brandon felt himself smiling at his mother, appreciating her more than he ever imagined.

"Are you sure you're both all right?" she asked when they'd finished their meals and dessert.

"It was wonderful, thank you," Anna said.

"Now are you going to tell us what the hell is going on?" Asa demanded.

Shelby shot him a warning look.

"I think we'd all like to know," J.T. said.

Brandon nodded and looked over at Anna. He covered her hand with his own and smiled reassuringly at her. "Like I said, it's a long story. And as far as we know, it doesn't have an ending yet."

CASH FOUND Dr. and Mrs. Porter Ivers in the master bedroom. Like all the other rooms, this one was spotlessly neat. The window next to the bed was open, the curtains billowing on the night breeze, the air fresh after the rainstorm.

Dr. Porter Ivers lay on the bed, his wife Emily in his arms, the two locked in an embrace.

Cash didn't need to check their pulses to know that they were both dead, but he did before he picked up the phone beside the bed to call Coroner Raymond Winters.

Beside the phone was an empty bottle of pills. Next to it was a glass half full of water. Propped against the night side lamp were two envelopes—one with the words *Sheriff Cash McCall* written on it, the other with simply *Taylor.*

Chapter Fifteen

Anna spent the night in the guest bedroom at the Sundown Ranch. Dusty brought her a white cotton nightgown.

"I'm sorry about your mother," the youngest McCall said as she gently laid the nightgown on the end of the guest bed, smoothing the fabric with her fingers. "I didn't have a mother, either." She turned and looked at Anna. "Well, until recently," she said with an eye roll.

"It's tough growing up without a mother," Anna agreed. "But you have one now."

Dusty shrugged. "Just like you have your father now. Aren't you mad at him, though, for what he did?"

Anna nodded and sat down on the edge of the bed, moving the nightgown so Dusty could join her. "I *am* angry. Part of the reason is that he lied to me for so long and I still don't know the truth."

"*Yeah,*" Dusty said, then lowered her voice

conspiratorially. "My parents told us why they did what they did to protect us. But we all know there's more. Like why she came back *now*, you know?"

Anna nodded.

"And how can I tell if they are telling me the truth now after they lied to me my whole life?" Dusty asked, sounding miserable.

"I guess all we can do is start somewhere. I want to know my father. I know there is good in him now. And he's family. You're lucky to have such a large family."

"But it sounds like you might have a sister," Dusty said.

Anna nodded, wondering how Taylor would take all of this. She hated to think. "I just know I don't want to waste any more time hating my father."

Dusty nodded and let out a long sigh. "It's just been so embarrassing, everyone in town talking about us." She mugged a face, then brightened. "But I guess they'll be talking about your family now." She caught herself, her eyes widening in horror. "Oh, I didn't mean—"

Anna laughed. "It's all right. If it takes away from people gossiping about your family, then something good has come out of it." Until the town got wind that Christianna VanHorn was with Brandon McCall. Even temporarily.

BRANDON COULDN'T sleep. He checked on Anna. She was tucked into the guest bedroom, asleep, breathing softly, reminding him of the nights they'd spent together; his sleepless one in the mountains and the amazing one at the lake cabin.

"I need to check on Cash," he told his mother. "Would you keep an eye—"

"On Anna? Of course." She seemed to study his face. "How serious is this, Brandon?"

He took a breath and let it out slowly. "On my part? Or hers?"

His mother nodded as if the answer was only too clear and patted his arm. "Go check on your brother."

He looked at her, seeing how beautiful she was now, thinking how pretty she must have been when she was even younger than Dusty.

"In high school," he began, "when Dad and VanHorn were both in love with you…" He swallowed.

"Was I in love with Mason?" she asked.

He nodded.

She smiled and seemed to choose her words carefully. "It was always Asa. Always. But if there hadn't been an Asa…" She sighed and met his gaze.

He let out the breath he'd been holding. "All

right." He backed toward the door. "Thank you for tonight."

"She's a beautiful, smart, capable young woman," Shelby said.

"Yeah, she is that."

ALL THE LIGHTS were on inside the sheriff's department. Brandon parked out front next to several state patrol cars. Several men were leaving as he walked in. Cash stood behind his desk, his back to the room.

"Did you get Ivers?" he asked.

Cash turned and nodded slowly.

Brandon could see by his face that something horrible had happened.

"He and Emily were dead when I got there," Cash said. "He left a confession."

"Does it clear Mason?" Brandon asked hopefully, thinking of Anna.

Cash nodded. "How are you?"

"Fine. Mason came out of surgery. Anna's out at the ranch."

"The Sundown?" he asked in surprise. "Asa must be beside himself."

"He took it pretty well," Brandon said. "But I don't think he'd be wild about having a Van-Horn for a daughter-in-law."

"Not that it matters what he wants. Is that something he should be worried about?"

"Anna and I…" He waved a hand through the air. "She thinks she wants to live on the home ranch. I think she won't last a month before she's ready for the city and her life back there."

"So it's like that," Cash said.

"Truthfully?" Brandon asked as he straddled a chair across from his brother's desk. "I don't know what it's like right now. So much has happened. I guess only time will tell."

"Have you told her you love her?" Cash asked as he pulled out his chair and sat down.

Brandon looked up at him in surprise.

"It's a place to start, little brother," Cash said with a smile. "Now, tell me what the hell's been going on."

Brandon started at the beginning with his job as night security on the VanHorn Ranch. Cash only interrupted a few times, usually just to swear or say, "What the hell were you thinking?"

From the job to the vandal to meeting Anna to finding out who she was and why she was in Montana, Brandon told him everything, including why Asa and Mason hated each other in the continuing feud of the McCalls and VanHorns.

"Mother?"

Brandon smiled and nodded. "She said if there hadn't been an Asa…" He told him about Anna's nanny and the deathbed confession, up until the part where Cash walked into Brookside.

"The nanny thought it had been Dr. French who delivered the babies and took Helena to Brookside," Brandon said. "The two were built the same, even about the same age, and Dr. Ivers said he used Dr. French's name when it suited him."

The phone rang. Cash answered it. "That was the hospital," he said after he hung up. "I can talk to Mason now. I still want a statement from you and Anna." He glanced at his watch. "Can the two of you stop by in the morning?"

THE NEXT MORNING, Anna left Brandon outside her father's hospital room while she went in.

Mason looked up, obviously surprised to see her. She went to him and planted a kiss on his weathered cheek. A tear rolled down. She brushed it away.

"I thought you would be gone back to Richmond," he said quietly. "I thought you would never want to see me again."

She pulled up a chair and sat down, taking his hand in both of hers. "I need to know the truth," she said, meeting his gaze. "No more lies."

He nodded and repeated the story he'd told her. "Ivers let me believe your mother killed that little baby."

"So you took it out to bury it," she said. "You didn't know she was having twins?"

He shook his head and looked down. "But when I came back in Ivers had called Niles French. French pulled me aside, I guess, so I didn't see Ivers leave. He was carrying something in his arms. I heard it cry. I knew there had been another baby...." He broke down for a moment. "God forgive me, but I didn't want that baby. Not a baby your mother had with another man, and I knew she wasn't able to take care of the two children we already had."

"So you knew Taylor was my sister?" Anna asked.

"No, I had no idea. I should have seen the resemblance, but Ivers let everyone believe his wife had been pregnant and had the baby early while staying at her sister's. Since the baby was a fraternal twin, it would have been premature."

Anna thought about her sister for a moment. "Dr. French took my mother to Brookside that night?"

He nodded. "I visited her every week. She didn't know who I was and sometimes she wouldn't even look at me, but I would talk to her and take pictures of you and Holt." Mason stopped, cleared this throat. "She was getting better...." Tears filled his eyes. "I adored your mother but she was always fragile."

"Cash says she was murdered in her room, 9B," Anna told him.

"Dr. French told me she was killed by another patient. He covered it all up, saying she was a Jane Doe he'd picked up off the highway and put in Brookside for the night. I still visit her grave and put flowers on it. Oh, Anna, I'm so sorry. I was a coward. If I'd only told the truth from the start...."

She squeezed his hand. "Did you kill Dr. French?"

His face hardened. "I realize now that Ivers killed your mother. She was getting better. She might have remembered the twins being born, she might have asked about the daughter who had lived."

Taylor. "His world was crumbling, his wife dying, me digging in the past," Anna said.

"He would have done anything to protect his daughter," Mason said. "I can understand that." He swallowed. "Your mother, in the days before she died, would look at the pictures I took her." He smiled through his tears. "She would touch the one of you and say how beautiful you were."

"I look like her."

He nodded. "I realize now it was the reason I pushed you away. I was afraid that I'd made

Helena the way she was. I feared…" He lowered his head, broke down.

She stood, leaning over him to press her lips into his hair. "I'm so sorry for all the horrible things I thought about you."

He wiped at his tears. "I am a hard man. Helena was the part of me that was soft and gentle. When I lost her…"

"Cash says you will probably get probation."

"I'm not worried about me." He drew back to look at her. "What will you do now?"

"I want to stay here." She met his gaze.

"McCall." He said it softly, then chuckled. "I guess I knew that day I saw the two of you sitting on that curb on Main Street. I thought if I sent you away…" He shook his head. "I thought the ranch and me made your mother sick. I wanted to free you from all of it. I guess it's always been your destiny."

"I hope so," Anna said.

BRANDON PUSHED OFF the wall where he'd been pacing back and forth as Anna came out of her father's room. There were tears in her eyes. "Is he all right?"

She nodded and bit her lower lip as Brandon reached for her. She came into his arms and he encircled her, burying his face in her dark hair.

She smelled like sunshine and rain and summer. He thought about what Cash had said. But this wasn't the place where he wanted to tell her he loved her.

The idea of telling her frightened him more than he wanted to admit. But he knew he had to do it, no matter the outcome. He couldn't let her leave Montana without knowing how he felt.

"I told Cash we'd stop by his office and give him our statements," he said.

She nodded against his chest, then pushed back, drying her eyes and taking a deep breath. She let it out slowly. "I'm ready."

CASH WAS on the phone in his office. They waited until he hung up to take the chairs he offered them.

"That was Lenore on the phone. She can't wait to get back to Richmond. She says she'll call you," Cash told Anna.

"I feel bad about what I put her through," Anna said.

"It comes with being a P.I. I'm sure she told you that." Cash leaned forward, turned on the tape recorder and took their statements. When they'd finished, he turned off the tape recorder and nodded. "Your stories fit what Dr. Ivers left in his confession and what Mason VanHorn told me."

"Have you talked to Taylor?" Anna asked. "Is she all right?"

Cash nodded. "According to Taylor, her father had been planning to take his wife's life and his own. That's why she came back to Antelope Flats."

"But she just learned that her father was a murderer," Anna said.

"No," Cash corrected her, "Taylor just learned that her father was Mason VanHorn."

Anna stared at the sheriff. "But my father said—"

"Your father was wrong. Taylor had suspected for some time that she wasn't Porter and Emily's biological daughter. It didn't add up. Mason was in the clinic a few months ago for a checkup. He showed both senior and junior Dr. Ivers a photograph of you, Anna. Taylor saw the resemblance—and the way her father reacted. She took some DNA when she did your father's checkup."

Anna was flabbergasted. "So my mother hadn't had an affair. But my father believed—"

"Your mother was very sick. I think Dr. Ivers knew the truth," Cash said. "That's why he was so afraid when a private investigator showed up asking a lot of questions. The night security woman saw Dr. Ivers and Josh Davidson bring Lenore into Brookside; she didn't know Ivers's real name. He'd told her it was French. But after she'd seen him lock Lenore in 9B... It wasn't her night to work. The other security watchman became suspicious when Davidson asked him a lot of questions about when he would be working and asked Emma Ingles to fill in for him. He later quit and left town. But it cost Emma her life."

Brandon reached over and took Anna's hand. "But you think Mason will get off with probation?"

"Probably," Cash said. "He and Dr. French did cover up your mother's death and your little brother's, as well as keep her stay at Brookside a secret. But the real crimes were committed by Dr. Ivers."

"Ivers killed Dr. French?" Brandon asked.

Cash nodded. "French wanted to come clean. He had been trying to get Helena's file from your father, Anna. He needed it to prove what had really happened. I guess he had cancer and wanted to confess all before he died."

"And Dr. Ivers couldn't let him," Brandon said. "Why did he just keep Lenore at Brookside and not get rid of her permanently?"

"Ultimately, Ivers was buying as much time as he could with his wife. I don't think he wanted to kill anyone." Cash leaned forward, putting his arms on the desk. "You might as well hear this from me. It will soon be common knowledge in Antelope Flats the way the gossip mill works here. Taylor wasn't the only baby Ivers took. You remember the Arnolds, Brandon?"

"Leticia's mom and dad?" Leticia was his sister Dusty's best friend.

"They wanted a baby desperately. I guess Leticia's mom was an unwed teenager," Cash said. "There are other babies Ivers stole. We're not sure how many."

"Does Leticia know?" Brandon asked.

Cash shook his head. "She doesn't know yet. It's one of the things I have to do before the day is over. Are you all right, Anna?"

She nodded, surprised that she was.

"Taylor says she'll stay in Antelope Flats and take over the clinic," Cash said. "I think in time she'll be glad she has a sister."

"Maybe someday," Anna said. "Right now, maybe I can just be a friend. She's going to need someone."

"That day at the clinic," Brandon said. "I saw her frowning as we left. I thought she was frowning at me, but she knew then that you were her sister."

Anna nodded. "I remember while she was checking my injury that she kept staring at me. Funny, but I did notice her eyes and thought how much they were like mine."

The phone rang. Cash answered, "Sure. Okay. All right." He hung up and looked at Anna and Brandon. "That was Shelby. She has called a family dinner. Tonight. Everyone is to be there." He raised a brow. "Who knows what's up now? But she said you're to bring Anna."

BRANDON DROVE Anna out to the lake to get her things. She was quiet on the drive. As they started up the steps of the cabin, he stopped her.

"Let's take a walk down by the lake first," he said, not wanting to see her pack her bags. Not yet, anyway.

She looked a little surprised, but agreed.

The lake was glass, the morning sun golden in a cloudless blue sky. The air smelled of pine and water and summer. He breathed it in, reminded of the summers he'd spent on the lake with his dad and brothers—and eventually his little sister. This was where he wanted his children to be raised. This was home—this valley, this life.

As he walked with Anna along the sandy beach, he realized that not long ago he'd wanted to escape it. To go to law school, knowing he probably wouldn't be back.

How could things have changed so much for him in a few days? He knew the answer. He'd never been in love before, didn't realize what a strong pull it exerted over him. Now he wanted to make new roots, to build a family, to make a life for himself here.

"There's something I have to tell you," he said and stopped to take both of her hands in his. He looked into her dark eyes, startled at how beautiful she was. "I love you."

The words were out so quickly, he surprised himself. He chuckled. "I had intended to say it more eloquently than that."

"Oh, I thought that was wonderfully eloquent," she said, her gaze locked with his.

He let go of her hands to pull off his Stetson and rake a hand through his hair. "I know this is sudden."

She laughed. "Sudden? You call twenty-two years sudden?" She cupped his face in her hands. "I fell for you that day on the curb, Brandon McCall. Do you know my father saw us together? It's another reason he sent me away. He was afraid I'd end up a ranchwoman."

"Oh." He felt all the wind come out of him.

She shook her head. "I told you that stupid

feud wasn't going to keep me from what I wanted. I told you what I've always wanted. You, and to get back to Montana. Ranching is in my blood. Anyway, my father knows how I feel about you."

"And?"

"And," she said smiling, "he said it must have been destiny."

"Destiny?" Brandon laughed. "I'm not sure that's what Asa is going to say."

"Don't worry, I'll win him over," she said and put her arms around him to gaze up into his face.

Brandon sighed. "Well, I guess tonight will be the night."

Chapter Sixteen

Anna spent the afternoon in Brandon's arms inside the cabin. They made love, talked, made love again, and talked some more. Suddenly, it seemed there was so much they had to say.

Until finally she laughed and said, "We have time to learn everything, don't we?" He hadn't asked her to marry him. And the one thing they seemed to have avoided talking about was her family ranch. She wondered if she was wrong about the two of them being able to overcome the feud between their families.

She wanted desperately to live on her ranch. That's how she'd thought of it since she had been a girl, when she used to ride her horse across the far reaches of it with her father. No one understood better than she did that feeling of ownership. Land was something solid to build on.

She knew she couldn't bring up the subject

herself because she still had to talk to her father about what she wanted. He knew she wanted this way of life. He didn't know she wanted the ranch. Not yet, anyway.

"Could we stop by the hospital on the way to dinner?" she asked. "I need to see my father again."

MASON VANHORN was awake, sitting up a little in his bed. His face brightened to see her walk in. He glanced toward the door. "You can bring McCall in with you. I won't bite off his head."

She smiled at that. "I wanted to talk to you alone. It's about the future. I don't want to go back to Richmond. I want to stay on the ranch."

He nodded. "You want to marry Brandon McCall and stay on the ranch."

"Yes."

"Even knowing how our families have battled for generations?" he asked.

"It was a silly feud." She regretted the words when she saw his pained expression. "You loved her, didn't you?"

"Your first love is hard to get over," Mason said.

Didn't she know it.

"I can't forgive Asa for taking her and making her so unhappy she left and lied about her death," Mason said.

"You don't know what happened between them," Anna said. "They're together now. I've seen them. They're happy."

He studied her a moment. "And you're happy with...Brandon."

She smiled at the way he said *Brandon* because she could see him coming around. "What were you going to do with the ranch if Holt didn't come back?"

"Holt isn't coming back. He's never had any interest in the ranch."

"So you were going to leave it to posterity?"

He laughed. "That does sound like me, doesn't it." He shook his head. "I was going to leave it to you. I didn't like to think what you would do with it. Sell it, I suppose." He met her gaze. "You want it, though."

She nodded. "More than almost anything else in life."

"Except Brandon McCall."

She smiled. "Except Brandon McCall."

"I liked building it up better than I ever liked running the ranch. It's yours, Anna. Lock, stock and barrel."

She couldn't hide her joy as she planted a kiss on her father's cheek.

"I'll have the papers drawn up right away," he said.

"I'd like it as a wedding present."

He raised a brow. "You're that sure this cowboy of yours is going to ask you to marry him?"

"Yes," she fibbed.

"I guess we'll see if McCall has any sense," Mason grumbled. "There is a great spot on some land to the north for a house."

She smiled. "You get well. I'm going to need you to walk me down the aisle. Only you won't be giving me away. You'll be welcoming me home."

Mason's eyes welled with tears. He cleared his throat. "Well, don't leave this man of your dreams out in the hall. Tell him to come in here."

"He hasn't asked me to marry him yet," she said quickly.

"Don't worry, I won't embarrass you," Mason said.

Anna called Brandon into the room. He looked gunshy but who could blame him?

"Brandon," Mason said. "I wanted to thank you for taking care of my daughter. She's really something, isn't she?"

"Yes, she is," Brandon said.

Mason nodded, watching the two of them.

"We really need to get going," Anna said. "We're having dinner with Brandon's family."

Mason raised a brow. "I'm sure you'll let me know how that goes. I'd say give Asa my best—"

"Let's not go there," Anna said, dragging Brandon back into the hall. She laughed at his expression.

"He hates me," Brandon said in the hallway.

"No, he doesn't," she assured him.

"Right. And now we have to face my entire family. You could probably use a stiff drink."

"It's going to be fine," she assured him.

He just nodded and she could tell he was worried. "Let me tell you about McCall family dinners. The last one my father called us together for, right in the middle of it, my mother showed up from the dead."

She laughed and hugged him. "I'm sure tonight will be fine."

He didn't look convinced.

BRANDON WAS RELIEVED that when they reached the Sundown Ranch house, everyone else had already arrived. Clearly, his mother had briefed them all on Anna.

A few were on the porch. Brandon made the introductions. "This is my brother Rourke and his wife Cassidy." Cassidy was very pregnant and more beautiful than he'd ever seen her. Cassidy had made the announcement of their happy news not too long ago.

"You've already met J.T.," Brandon said. "This is his wife Regina."

"Reggie," Regina corrected and grinned at her husband. "It's wonderful to meet you, Anna. Do you ride?"

"She's a wonderful horsewoman," Brandon said, everyone hearing the pride in his voice—including Anna. She blushed and looked embarrassed.

"I'm still trying to learn," Reggie said. "Maybe someday you could give me some pointers."

"I'd like that," Anna said.

"Does that mean you're staying in Antelope Flats?" J.T. asked.

Brandon looked at Anna. She smiled. "Yes," she said.

Inside the house, Dusty greeted Anna like a long-lost sister, and Shelby swept Anna away to the kitchen.

Asa and Cash had been sitting in front of the fireplace. Brandon was surprised to see that there was a small fire burning. The house felt hot, but Asa was in the chair closest to the blaze. Brandon felt a stab of worry.

"Hello, son," Asa said and motioned to a

chair near him. "Cash was just telling me about old Doc Ivers. Isn't that somethin'? Who would have ever suspected him of such things."

Unlike Mason VanHorn, Brandon thought. "It was a horrible set of events. Especially for Mason. And Anna."

"Yes," Asa said, his eyes narrowing. "You brought her with you to dinner?"

"Mother insisted," Brandon said carefully.

"Mother, is it now?" Asa said, then nodded. "I'm glad to hear it."

Cash got to his feet and, turning his back to their father, inclined his head as if to say, "Talk to him."

"I need to check on Molly. I think Mother has her cooking something. A frightening thought," Cash said.

"Your brother never has been subtle," Asa said as he watched Cash leave. "So what is it you want to talk to me about?" he asked, turning to look at his youngest son.

"I'm in love with her," Brandon said simply.

"Any fool can see that. But do you know what you're getting into? She's a *VanHorn*." Asa shook his head. "No good can come of it."

Brandon heard the familiar words and found himself smiling. "I've heard that all my life when it came to the VanHorns and the McCalls.

But you're wrong. I love her and I'm going to ask her to marry me. If she says yes, then I'm hoping to make you and Mason grandfathers. What do you think about that?" Brandon demanded, leaning toward his father, daring him to say the wrong thing.

To his surprise, his father began to laugh. "I wondered how long it would take you to be your own man. It's about damned time." He reached for his son's hand and shook it, his grip not as strong as Brandon remembered it.

"Dinner's served," his mother called from behind them.

When Brandon turned, he saw tears in her eyes. She quickly brushed them away and reached for his hand. She pressed something into it and whispered. "It belonged to my grandmother."

Everyone filed into the dining room. Brandon hung back, staring down at the small velvet box and the pretty simple diamond ring inside.

He looked up at the sound of Anna's laughter. She came down the hallway from the kitchen, joking with Molly. She stopped walking when she saw him.

"Sit by me at dinner," Molly said, and gave Brandon a grin as she entered the dining room.

Everyone else was inside except Brandon and Anna. The double doors were open and he could see them all pretending not to watch.

"I have no idea what my mother plans to announce tonight at dinner, but I know what I'd like it to be," Brandon said as he looked into Anna's dark eyes.

Taking a breath, he pulled off his Stetson and dropped to one knee. "Would you marry me?"

Anna's eyes filled with tears as he held out the diamond.

"It belonged to my great-grandmother, I'm told," he said.

Anna blinked, then brushed at her tears and sniffled as she threw herself into his arms. "Yes, oh, yes!" she cried, knocking him over backward.

The dining room erupted in applause.

For a few moments, Brandon lay sprawled on the floor with his future bride. Then he slipped the diamond onto her finger—not all that surprised when it fit perfectly. Some things really were destined.

He kissed her, losing himself until he heard his father clear his throat.

Getting up, Brandon helped Anna to her feet. They brushed themselves off and entered the dining room as if nothing had happened.

When they were seated, his mother looked

over at Asa and started to speak, but Asa took her hand and shook his head. "Tonight, we celebrate."

She looked at her husband for a long moment, then nodded and smiled as she glanced around the table.

"Is there something going on we should know about?" J.T. asked, looking worried.

"We don't have enough of these family dinners," Asa said, sounding a little choked up. "You kids always think something is going on. Everything is wonderful," he said, looking around the table. His gaze lighted on Anna. He looked worried for a moment, then cleared his throat and said, "Welcome to the family."

"I GET TO HELP with the wedding," Dusty said eagerly as everyone raised a glass to the engaged couple.

Martha appeared in the doorway. "Ty Coltrane is here. He just wanted you to know he left the horses you bought in the pen, Asa."

"Tell that boy to come in here and have some dinner," Asa hollered. "Martha, get another place setting."

"Sir, I didn't mean to interrupt your dinner," said the lanky, good-looking young cowboy in the doorway. "I should be getting home." The young man's gaze went straight to Dusty. His mouth fell open a little at just the sight of her.

"Dusty, make some room for him," Asa ordered. "Brandon, get another chair. Of course, he's joining us."

Dusty glared at her father. "He just said he couldn't stay for dinner."

"Nonsense," Asa said. Dusty was his last. She was young and stubborn. All she needed was a good man. Not that he would ever say that to Shelby. She'd have his hide.

"Well, thank you, sir," Ty Coltrane said. "I wouldn't mind joining your family for dinner if you're sure it's not an inconvenience."

"None at all." Asa smiled at his wife. She was giving him one of her warning looks. He'd never listened to good advice in all his years. No reason to start now.

Dusty was giving him her don't-do-it-or-you'll-regret-it look. Asa smiled as Ty enthusiastically drew up a chair next to Dusty.

"Now," Asa said as he looked around the table. "Let's have dinner."

Dusty shot him the always-popular teenager's I'm-never-speaking-to-you-again look. He chuckled to himself. He could use the peace and quiet.

Shelby reached over, took his hand and

squeezed it, shaking her head as if he were the most incorrigible man she'd ever met. He sure as hell was.

He squeezed back, savoring this moment in time. He had tonight and he was damned sure going to enjoy it. "To the McCalls," he thought to himself, and raised his glass in a silent salute.

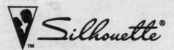